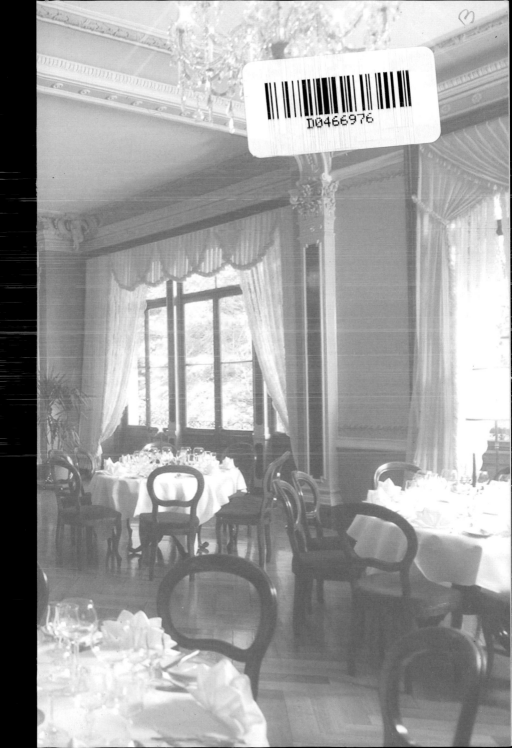

A Perfect Waiter

A Novel

Alain Claude Sulzer

Translated from the German
by John Brownjohn

BLOOMSBURY

swiss arts council
prohelvetia

Published by Bloomsbury USA, New York
Distributed to the trade by Macmillan

All papers used by Bloomsbury USA are natural, recyclable products made from wood grown in well-managed forests. The manufacturing processes conform to the environmental regulations of the country of origin.

LIBRARY OF CONGRESS CATALOGING-IN-PUBLICATION DATA HAS BEEN APPLIED FOR

ISBN-10 1-59691-411-4
ISBN-13 978-1-59691-411-7

Originally published in German as *Ein perfekter Kellner* by Edition Epoca in 2004
First U.S. Edition 2008

1 3 5 7 9 10 8 6 4 2

Typeset by Hewer Text UK Ltd, Edinburgh
Printed in the United States of America by Quebecor World Fairfield

Apart, who can divide us?
Divided, we shall never be parted.

Twilight of the Gods
Richard Wagner

I

On September 15, 1966, Erneste was surprised to receive a letter from New York. But there was no one with whom he could have shared his feelings. He was alone—there was no one to whom he could have confided how utterly astonished and delighted he was to hear from Jakob, the friend he hadn't seen since 1936. His dearest wish, which was that Jakob might someday return from the place he had gone to thirty years earlier, had never been fulfilled. Now he was standing in front of his mailbox with Jakob's letter in his hand. He turned it this way and that, staring at the stamp as intently as if he had to memorize the number of lines in the postmark running across it, until he finally put the envelope in his breast pocket.

Erneste seldom received any mail. Getting a letter from Jakob, whom he had completely lost sight of but never forgotten, was more than he'd dared to hope for in recent years. Jakob wasn't dead, as he had sometimes feared; Jakob was alive—still alive and living in America. Jakob had written to him.

There hadn't been a day in all these years when Erneste had failed to think of Jakob. He had lost sight of him, yes, but he'd never erased him from his memory. The past was locked away in his abundant recollections of Jakob like something inside a dark closet. The past was precious, but the closet remained unopened.

———•———

Erneste gave the tablecloth a quick wipe with his napkin. The crumbs went flying, but none landed on the dress of the young woman who was deep in conversation with a somewhat older man in a dark-blue suit. From the couple's awkward manner, Erneste felt sure she was appearing in public with him for the first time. Having been a fixture at the Restaurant am Berg for sixteen years, Erneste was the most dependable member of an ever-changing staff. Never once ill or absent in all that time, he had seen countless waiters and waitresses, chefs and kitchen hands, subordinates and superiors come and go, whereas he himself was known—and had no objection to being known—as a rock in shifting sands. He was a reserved, rather pallid man of medium height and indeterminate age with the impeccable manners of a patient and perceptive employee—almost a gentleman. He accepted his tips with even-handed dignity and hoarded them with care, never tempted to live above his means.

Shadowlike when he had to be, Erneste was also an attentive observer who would come hurrying up at the right moment, thoroughly alert and quick on the uptake.

Equipped with a more than adequate command of German, Italian, English, and—of course—French, since France was his native land, unobtrusive but omnipresent Erneste was a man of whom little was known. No diner ever dreamed of asking Monsieur Erneste what his surname was. He lived in a small apartment, two furnished rooms rented for 280 Swiss francs a month.

Erneste liked being a waiter and had never aspired to any other profession. Just then he caught sight of a little glistening bead of sweat on the man's moist neck, a few millimeters above his collar. Nauseated, not that he showed it, he turned away with an impassive expression. Someone had raised a hand and called his name. He hurried over, gave a little bow, and proceeded to clear the table. The diners, an architect and his wife and a young couple unknown to him, requested some cheese and another bottle of wine.

For years now, Erneste had waited table exclusively in the Blue Room. This part of the Restaurant am Berg differed markedly from the outer room, a smoky rendezvous patronized by the younger set: artists and students, actors and their fans, quaffers of beer and Beaujolais. None of Erneste's superiors, not even the manager himself, would have dared to ask him to wait table in the Brown Room. He was responsible only for the Blue Room, the one with the pale-blue drapes, where dinner was served punctually between seven and ten, not a moment before or after, every day except Sundays. No one who did not intend to eat was admitted before ten o'clock at night. Even Monsieur Erneste could prove severe in that respect.

Monsieur Erneste belonged to a dying breed and he knew it, but he had no idea whether the people he waited on with due *courtoisie* knew it too. Wondering about it would have been a waste of time. But they, too, were members of a dying breed. Erneste didn't know if they realized it. Perhaps they merely sensed that they were growing older by degrees. The knowledge that they were not yet decrepit lent them the requisite sense of security. They had yet to resemble their elderly parents, who languished someplace in the country or the suburbs, where their offspring never made an effort to visit them except on Sundays. Such were Erneste's thoughts as he turned to go and order a bottle of Château Léoville Poyferré 1953, four glasses, and *les fromages*: Camembert and Reblochon, the best possible cheeses to accompany the wine in question. Plenty of things would change here too, but less drastically, no doubt, than elsewhere. Erneste wasn't blind. On the contrary, he had good eyesight and an excellent memory, and not just for the orders he took.

Erneste was entirely devoted to his profession. He had left home at sixteen, desperately eager to get away from his native village, his parents and his brothers and sisters, who had detected something alien and repellent in him. He went off to Strasbourg and became a waiter. He loved his profession because it brought him the freedom he'd craved for so long, the ability to do and think whatever he pleased without being observed. In that regard, nothing had changed since his first job thirty-five years ago. He was free. He wasn't wealthy, but he was a free agent. He didn't know whether his siblings were still alive, but they probably were, since they weren't much older or younger than himself. At some stage—how many years ago was it?—they had informed him of his father's death. His mother had died a few months later, but he didn't respond or attend the funeral. Her image had faded long before. He hadn't acknowledged the death notice.

Nobody knew who he was. No one was interested, no one cared about his private life. When diners asked how he was they were merely uttering a form of salutation. "And how are *you?*" he would reply as he took their coats—a question that would have been wholly out of order back at the Grand Hotel, where a waiter talked with guests only in response to a direct inquiry but preferably not at all. Still, a restaurant wasn't a hotel, and besides, times had changed. The rules weren't quite as strictly observed these days.

The patrons of the Restaurant am Berg knew only that Erneste was an Alsatian. This was obvious, but they didn't call him an Alsatian; they referred to him as a Frenchman even though his accent was unmistakably Alemannic, not French. How old was he? Over forty and under sixty, but he was such a staple part of the restaurant's inventory that no one devoted any more thought to his age than they did to the true age or authenticity of the various pieces of furniture that had always stood there, which were, of course, Louis Quinze or Biedermeier reproductions. And he himself felt a part of that inventory. After all, he knew every plate, every knife and fork, every napkin, every irregularity in the parquet floor, every fringe of every carpet, every picture, every vase. Being reputed to have an artistic eye, Erneste was responsible for the restaurant's floral decorations.

He was indifferent to the days of the week. They came and went as he worked and he worked as they came and went, each as unmomentous as the next. He took little notice of the seasons. In springtime he exchanged his heavier overcoat for the lighter one, in wintertime his lighter overcoat for the heavier one, and that was that. First came spring, then winter. In the intervening periods he made do with jackets, two dark and one pale. He never wore cardigans. On Sunday, his only day off, he slept in, often until noon. He savored the peace and quiet and thought of his next working day, listening to classical music on the radio—operatic arias and lieder for choice. Choral music he liked less, but he never turned a program off and stayed with it to the end. He had never been to the opera, even though his salary would have enabled him to afford the occasional theater ticket. He had seen singers visit the restaurant and noted their names, but they never stayed long because they couldn't stand the cigarette smoke. They didn't smoke themselves, drank nothing but mineral water, and said little.

So Erneste contented himself with lightweight fare such as Adolphe Adam's comic opera *Le Postillon de Longjumeau.* He was happy listening to the radio in his warm bed. He was alone but he didn't feel lonely—or only sometimes. That was when destructive thoughts coursed through him, only to disappear as quickly as they had come. He didn't abandon himself to them, nor did they haunt him. When he took a vacation, which was seldom, he usually spent it in the mountains. He had also been once to the Loire Valley and once each to Venice and Biarritz. The better rooms of the little hotel in Biarritz were already taken, unfortunately, so he'd had no view of the sea, but it was audible day and night.

Erneste sometimes went out after work on Saturdays, except that then he ran the risk of drinking too much. He didn't like making a fool of himself, which wasn't always easy at his age. Once he started drinking he couldn't stop—he simply couldn't help it. He had a recurrent dream in which a gang of schoolkids demanded to see his identity card, which he either didn't possess or wasn't carrying, and when they saw he couldn't produce it they got angry, and no one restrained them. Incapable of defending himself, he was glad to wake up.

Only two bars came into consideration when he went out. He seldom encountered any patrons of the Restaurant am Berg there. If he did, he would say a polite hello but avoid getting into conversation on the principle that one's leisure time and professional duties were mutually exclusive. If he encountered them at the restaurant he showed no sign of recognition, although their faces belied this. He occasionally smoked a cigarette or two in one of the bars, which didn't close until three in the morning, and chatted there with strangers or casual acquaintances. At other times he spoke to nobody and nobody spoke to him. Afterward he would set off for home on his own. When he emerged into the open the cold morning air enveloped him like an intimate embrace, a dank, agreeable penumbra that reminded him of Paris, although it smelled quite different here. As he slowly skirted the lake and made his way along the river bank, the moisture seeped gradually through his clothes to the skin. He liked that too. He was free, exempt from any commitments outside his job. He never paused, always walked on, trying to think of nothing at all. Then he dreamed.

———————

There was no hurry. He let two days go by before he finally decided to open the letter during the early hours of Sunday morning. He gave his imagination free rein while he waited table, thinking of the letter. By not opening it he brought time to a halt. He didn't read it on Friday, nor on Saturday. The time he brought to a halt—the time concealed in the envelope—burned through his waiter's dickey and seared his chest. He carried the letter around for two whole days. At night he put it on the bedside table and fell asleep looking at it—a titillating pleasure. He brought time to a standstill by not opening the letter, not yet. He waited, trying to imagine what was in it.

The letters he had received in the last ten years could be counted on the fingers of both hands. Customers didn't write, colleagues wrote to the entire staff, and of friends he had none. Any mail he received consisted of bills or circulars, Christmas mail-order catalogs advertising watercolors by disabled artists, some clumsily executed, others painted with surprising skill, using the feet or the mouth, and an occasional postcard from his cousin in Paris.

He put off reading the letter until he felt he knew its unseen contents. For two whole days, from Friday morning until the early hours of Sunday, his thoughts revolved almost exclusively around this unopened letter from America, this rare excitement in a life so devoid of it. All his emotions were centered on the envelope and its contents. Whatever he did he did mechanically, thinking of the letter inside, of the long-written, still unread words penned by the same hand that had inscribed his address in unfamiliar capitals, for the Jakob that Erneste knew had never written to him. At the Grand Hotel there was no need, and Jakob had deemed it just as unnecessary to write to him later on. In the room they shared, the rushing waters of the Giessbach had drowned all other sounds. Erneste could still hear them after all this time.

"Monsieur Erneste!" Erneste hurried over to the table with the check. He took the money and the tip, pulled back the lady's chair and stepped aside, helped her into her coat, then her male companion.

If his expression suddenly brightened, illumined by the ghost of a smile, it surely passed unnoticed. The couple were preoccupied with themselves, which was just as it should be. Under no circumstances should patrons be given cause to concern themselves with those whose task it was to attend to their wellbeing. His thoughts had strayed because they were constantly revolving around Jakob's letter, but that remained a secret he was unable and unwilling to share with anyone else. The letter was like a hand reaching for him, its pressure neither heavy nor light. Two days of waiting, two days' delay, were not a waste of time, not a symptom of reluctance—no, of joyful expectancy. He wasn't afraid, or not yet. He wasn't overcome by a vague feeling of apprehension until just before he opened the letter. His imagination was still as nourished by uncertainty about its contents as a hungry man by the prospect of a slice of meat.

Two days were long enough. Erneste could endure it no longer. He reached for the morsel, eager to devour it.

———·•·———

He wasted no time drinking in bars on Saturday night. Although he couldn't see well in the darkness, he wore no glasses. He was slightly out of breath. Jakob had something to tell him; now he wanted to know what it was. He debated the question while walking home from work. "Has Jakob written to *me* or only in general terms?" he wondered. "Has he written from his new world to our old world in order to give it something it doesn't possess? Would you recognize me on the street, Jakob, now that our youth is long past and bereft of interest, and would I recognize you? Probably not. We'd pass by without a second glance, like two men who have never seen each other before." He was fraught with recollections of a young man. Happiness was easily acquired and quickly lost.

Home by a quarter to one, he opened the door of his apartment and a bottle of Scotch, in that order.

His hands were trembling. He poured himself another glass, filled it to the brim and drained it in two gulps, then deposited the bottle on the dresser behind him. He often sat in his little kitchen, where there was nothing to distract him. He didn't possess a television set. When, discounting Sundays, would he have had the time to take advantage of such an expensive acquisition? The 500 francs in his savings book wouldn't have stretched to a TV.

Impatience and curiosity were one thing, but courage was required to satisfy them. That he had now obtained from a bottle like someone having to confront a stranger, a prospective employer, or an unwelcome visitor who would persist in ringing his doorbell until he answered it. He had to open the door, there was no alternative. Yes, now he was afraid.

When the time came to open the letter at last, he wondered if it wouldn't be better to destroy it after all—to throw it away unread like an empty husk. After all the years in which he had never forgotten Jakob, a letter from him boded no good. So confidence was out of place, as was the pleasurable anticipation that had buoyed him up for the past two days. A letter from Jakob boded no good, period. Another drink. Half a glass, a whole glass. He hesitated briefly, then filled his glass to the brim and put the bottle down beside him. Danger lurked in this rustling envelope. It would lunge at him in a moment, and he was unprepared. But what was the point of waiting? As soon as curiosity triumphed over common sense—the common sense that told him: "Don't open it, throw it away, don't look at it!"—his old wounds would open up again. He knew this but was incapable of obeying the dictates of caution. The letter would reopen his scars once more— letters could do that. He was far more afraid of the words that awaited him than of the futile passage of time.

He sat there in the kitchen in his shirtsleeves, alive but inwardly extinct. In this get-up he was a man. Normally recognizable as a waiter only by his white linen jacket, he became an individual without one. As a waiter he was a nobody, which was just as it should be, but the jacket had to be clean and well pressed. He looked up. His gaze lingered on the only lighted window in the apartment house across the street. By now it was half-past one. A shadow stirred in the glow—it rose and fell, rose abruptly and disappeared into the adjoining room. That room was in darkness. Erneste had never seen a light on in there— the bedroom, probably. He was familiar with the shadowy figure of the sleepless woman who hurried back and forth, bobbed up and down, but he didn't know her name and had never seen her face. He had no idea what she did, whether she read or knitted, had never seen her on the street and wouldn't have recognized her if he had. She had no television. The light was on, night after night, whenever he came home from work. The window of that one room was always illuminated, as now. The light did not go out for days after she died, but that happened weeks later.

Would the letter contain a photo of Jakob? He had preserved the few photos of Jakob he possessed, snapshots with serrated edges, so carefully that he'd almost forgotten about them. He had stowed them away in a box and deposited the box in the cellar. They were out of reach, as remote as Jakob's breath and even more remote than the memories of their time together at Giessbach. He never looked at old photos. Old photos only provoked gloomy thoughts of the present.

But he was secretly hoping for more than just words—for a portrait, a photograph of Jakob. Had time played havoc with his face? Had it been as unfair, implacable and incorruptible as it usually was? Had it ravaged Jakob's face as well as his own, so that he tended to look away when confronted by his reflection in a mirror? Whatever was in the envelope on the table in front of him, it certainly wasn't a photograph. His fingers would have detected a photograph through the airmail paper.

And then, at long last, he proceeded to open the letter. He didn't use a knife or scissors, he slit it open with the little finger of his right hand. The paper was so thin, a single movement sufficed to open the envelope, which rustled softly and tore. How Jakob had obtained his address was a mystery to which he'd already given some thought. He withdrew the letter, a single sheet folded three times, from the envelope. Unlike the address, the letter itself had been typed. In many places the typewriter had pierced the paper and left tiny fissures and protrusions on the back of the sheet. Only the signature was handwritten, but the "Jakob" in the sender's address on the back of the envelope had been replaced by "Jack" carelessly scrawled in slanting letters and terminating in a silly little squiggle. All this Erneste took in at a glance after unfolding the letter and before he'd read a single word of it. He felt that everything hitherto had been merely a dream, and now he was waking up.

What he read was the diametrical opposite of what he had secretly been hoping for the last two days: that Jakob had changed. He hadn't. Jakob was the same as ever, whether he called himself Jakob or Jack: interested solely in his own concerns. Erneste's throat became more and more parched as he scanned the shatteringly impersonal, unambiguous lines again and again, but he didn't take a drink—he couldn't. It never even occurred to him to reach for the bottle beside him. Reading the words addressed to him again and again, he failed at first to grasp their meaning; then he grasped it only too well. And, even as he still sought to persuade himself that this Jack couldn't possibly be the Jakob who had once been so close to him, the one with whom he'd shared the attic room in Giessbach, he naturally realized that no one other than this far-off Jakob, transmogrified into Jack, had welded these words, this request, into the deadly projectile that

now smote him, Erneste, like a bullet from a gun. He saw
the lake before him, blue as ice and cold as slate. Its waters
rose and engulfed him—no, he was sinking, done for. He
was and remained alone, was and remained a ridiculous
individual. The request addressed to him appealed for
help but not for friendship. For reasons unknown to
Erneste, Jakob was banking on his assistance.

He had written:

Dear Erneste,

*It's ages since I wrote to you. You haven't written either, didn't
you have my address? I'm writing this from New York, where I've
been living for many years. Have you thought of me from time to
time? We're so far apart. Life is tough here, mainly because
everything has turned out differently than I imagined. I badly need
your help, I don't know where else to turn. Please go to Klinger for
me and ask him a favor, otherwise I'm finished. My financial
position is very shaky, and not just my financial position. You can
help me—you must help me! Please go to Klinger and ask him to
send me some money. Just tell him I'm in a bad way from every
angle. I went away with him that time, and now I wonder if it
wasn't a mistake. I survived the war over here, sure, but I never
managed to get back to Europe. They say K has been nominated for
the Nobel Prize, so he must have plenty of cash. I wanted to leave
everything behind me, but I didn't succeed, not altogether. I often
think of Cologne and my mother, who's dead now. You'll know
where to find K. He lives near you, as I'm sure you've heard. Please
write me when you've had a word with him. I doubt if I'll ever come
back. I could go back to Germany if I had the money, but who's got*

any money except him? Do you have any? Are you well off? Please keep me posted. He owes me, it's only right! Any chance I could come to Switzerland?

    All the best,
    Jack.

2

Erneste hadn't forgotten his arrival in Giessbach on April 2, 1934, or his first day at work there. Nor had he forgotten Jakob's arrival a year later, in May 1935, the beginning of a sojourn abroad to which Jakob probably owed his life. The young German's spell of employment in Switzerland had saved him from being drafted into the Wehrmacht, as he inevitably would have been if he'd stayed at home for the next four years. You didn't need to know much about politics in 1935 to guess what was to be expected from Germany if Hitler remained in power there. You had only to open one of the newspapers displayed in the hotel lobby or overhear some German or Austrian visitor talking. No matter what attitude individual guests adopted toward the new German regime— whether they endorsed or condemned it, whether they sought to understand or excuse, belittle or oppose it— everything indicated that the cataclysm of which so many people spoke had not been consummated by Hitler's accession to power but was really still to come. The fire had been kindled but had not yet burst into a blaze. The word "war" was on everyone's lips. It was said that

German policy would inevitably result in chaos and another millionfold bloodbath.

Erneste could still picture certain hotel guests after thirty years. A few names and faces had lodged in his mind. He pictured them in the morning, when they appeared in the breakfast room looking bleary, dazzled by the light and often unwashed. He pictured them, too, wide awake in the evening, when they entered the spacious dining room overlooking the Giessbach, eager for attention and recognition and thirsting for adventure where little or none was to be had, or, when the temperature permitted, sinking into the softly creaking wickerwork chairs on the terrace overlooking the lake, lighting their cigars or cigarettes or having them lighted if a waiter was nearby, ordering their cocktails, putting glasses filled with ice cubes to their lips, and broaching a preliminary bottle of wine, white before red. The waiters were run off their feet, and if several guests were seated at a table, further bottles would be opened as the evening wore on.

The guests dined and talked, drank and laughed, hailed new arrivals and took note of those who contrived to draw attention to themselves, scanned the room for acquaintances and waved to them. But it was considered bad form to change tables during dinner or even thereafter, so they remained seated. One could always meet up later on the terrace or in the hotel bar.

Particular interest was devoted to those who ate alone, especially on the first night of their stay. It was tactless to stare but impolite to ignore them. Those who benefited from a good vantage point could tell their table companions a great deal about such new arrivals. The majority of them were on the elderly side. Some drank nothing but water in a positively defiant manner, others visibly over-indulged themselves in port or sherry, many skimmed through newspapers or books before or after the meal or between courses, and most were at pains to make a nonchalant, abstracted impression. But few of them succeeded in grandly ignoring the other guests' surreptitious glances, and many such loners became more and more obviously insecure in the course of a meal. Hauteur made but a frail suit of armor when a person had to eat in solitary state.

The wealthier the guests, the more attention they were entitled to demand and the more attention people devoted to those aspects of their existence that should definitely have been exempt from public scrutiny. The private lives of some unaccompanied guests were a trifle disreputable. People suspected them of hiding something, so they never took their eyes off them. Thus, Erneste became acquainted with the characteristics of the beau monde, the social class that was wont to relax, untroubled by politics or business, in the hotel's luxurious ambience. It did not, however, escape him that few of the guests came from the very highest reaches of society, for the Grand Hotel's great days were over. Any aristocrats still to be seen in Giessbach were of junior status only.

Guests tended to keep to themselves. Some considered

themselves superior to others and let them feel it, the more unobtrusively, the more effectively. Within this setting, which was also populated by sundry eccentrics and unprepossessing bores, members of the hotel's omnipresent and indispensable staff were perceived only out of the corner of the eye, on the visual periphery. Since most of them were young, dark, and from Southern Europe, cases of mistaken identity were of almost daily occurrence. In order to make their mark, waiters had to be exceptionally attractive or unattractive in appearance. To most of the guests they all looked the same.

It was advisable to treat lone guests with particular consideration, not least because they were the best tippers. In contrast to married couples, who spent most of the day supervising their children, they were more inclined to converse with members of staff. They exchanged friendly words with them in the corridors, on the curving staircase, on the terrace in the morning, in the gardens in the afternoon. Such conversations tended to become protracted, so hotel employees would have to hurry to fulfill their other duties without making guests feel that they had detained them unnecessarily. These brief exchanges, which nearly always took place in public and were watched with interest, brought staff and guests somewhat closer, even though the social divide was always preserved. No one took exception to these chance encounters and brief chats. On the contrary, the management expressly encouraged members of staff to devote time to unaccompanied guests whenever possible.

A nod or a slight turn of the body sufficed to convey that a guest wished to terminate a conversation. The hotel employee had then to respond in an appropriate manner, neither precipitately nor too deliberately. He learned all these things, after committing the usual blunders, by experience and empathy. It was up to him to develop the proper sensitivity to a guest's wishes.

Lone guests had a predilection for chatting with waiters during meals in the dining room. This was when a few casual words on their part could best demonstrate the spurious nonchalance that was designed to conceal from their fellow guests how vulnerable they felt without a table companion. Aspiring waiters, in their turn, were thereby enabled to converse with denizens of another world of which they could never learn enough, for everything they learned helped them to treat the inhabitants of that other world with even greater understanding in the future. The better acquainted they were with their habits and body language, the more promptly and efficiently they could fulfill their requirements.

When requested to do so, as they were on rare occasions, waiters were even at liberty to touch upon personal matters. The management turned a blind eye to these intimacies, if they were noticed at all. A guest generally began by asking a waiter's age and place of origin, then his background and future plans, his family circumstances and whether he planned to marry soon or had no intention of marrying at all—inquiries fraught with an implicit interrogation mark. When asked such questions, which it wasn't really proper for a waiter to answer frankly, it took some practice for him not to blush, let alone tremble or spill something. Loud laughter was unseemly—not a ground for dismissal, but reason enough for the management to reprimand or subject him to unwelcome surveillance.

All these things were quickly learned. Erneste himself had learned them as quickly as Jakob was soon to do. One picked them up in passing, so to speak, and it nearly always paid off in the end. Lonely guests were generous when they left, not only with their tips but sometimes with their tears. Yes, Erneste had seen tears, some suppressed but others that flowed with relative abandon. Tears not only in the eyes of the bachelor whose face and name he'd forgotten, unlike the weight of his body, a Belgian nobleman *d'un certain âge* whose advances he had not rejected because he had no need to feel ashamed of himself on that account. Cold, clear tears, too, in the eyes of widows whose chagrin was not necessarily associated with one particular individual, still less with a humble hotel employee, but simply with the fact that their departure was inevitable, and that every departure, every farewell, denoted the end of something: the end of the summer, of pleasant evenings on the terrace, of strolls beside the Giessbach Falls, of leisurely boat trips across the Lake of Brienz to Interlaken, of a vacationer's existence. For what came after their vacation would be far worse than their present solitude. No one would be awaiting them on their return—no one, at least, who was eager to lavish affection on them; just their servants, their daily irritations and the eternal, monotonous routine of everyday life. But of this they spoke allusively at most. Who wanted to know the nature of their world-weariness? Most of them were tactful enough to refrain from burdening hotel employees with their woes, which probably stemmed from the very affluence for which the less affluent yearned.

Erneste had nothing to reproach himself for, nor had he deluded himself. The Belgian had wept, not for him but for himself. The tears he shed on that morning in early spring—a few tears only—had been shed, not for Erneste but for Erneste's youth and, thus, for the Belgian's age. They derived from the biological fact that a gulf yawned between them—one that nothing could bridge or offset, neither words nor physical contact nor money. Erneste was twenty or thirty years younger, and at that moment those years formed an even greater barrier than wealth between two men who shared the same secret. The young waiter had nothing, whereas the older man possessed all the makings of a pleasurable existence, but Erneste's youth outweighed that a hundred times over, whereas the Belgian's vanished youth could never be retrieved or bought back. Had he allowed it to pass him by? Erneste didn't know. He saw the man weep, nothing more, treating himself to nostalgia like the ring on his finger and the eau de Cologne on his skin. He couldn't regain his youth as he might have recouped a dud investment; he could only buy its semblance for a while—in this case, through the medium of a young man named Erneste. You didn't get any younger if you looked in the mirror; on the contrary, the younger your companion, the older you seemed to yourself. The Belgian had certainly never wondered how many years of his life the young waiter would have given for a small fraction of his money; that didn't interest him. He merely surrendered to the bitter-sweet pain of melancholy before departing a few hours later.

When the Belgian nobleman was leaving, Erneste felt briefly tempted to yield to an absurd impulse: to embrace him in front of everyone just as he was shaking hands with the manager in the hotel lobby. Instead, he took the bill he was given and bowed. But, when their eyes met, it was Erneste who triumphed. He was young, the other man old. He never forgot him, strangely enough. One thought was enough to conjure up a vision of the Belgian's body, though he couldn't remember his face. The lasting impression the Belgian had made on him was in stark contrast to the brevity of their relationship.

Hotel guests, whether bachelors, widows or married couples, could leave at any time, whereas Erneste and his colleagues had no choice but to await the arrival of more guests, who were not long in coming at the height of the season. In Erneste's memory thirty years later they had become fused into a faceless mass consisting mainly of clothes whose wearers were engaged in relaxing, sunbathing in the grounds, strolling around, going for little excursions, eating, drinking, smoking in the bar, and talking a great deal.

Erneste listened to them with only half an ear or not at all. Uninterested in politics, he concentrated on fulfilling their wishes. Hotel staff, whose political opinions it never occurred to anyone to ask, were employed to keep guests happy regardless of what was happening elsewhere. Although their own lives would certainly not be unaffected by political developments in the outside world, their job consisted solely in melting into the walls and wallpaper past which they bustled to and fro as briskly but silently as possible. They didn't advertise their personal opinions; that would have damaged the hotel's reputation. It was only natural, however, that many hotel employees had a relatively clear idea of the future that lay in store for them if war broke out. The majority hoped someday to be able to return home with their savings, there to embark on a new life entirely different from that of their neighbors, who would continue to live in penury for the rest of their days. Erneste was a stranger to such dreams. His own dream had already come true. He would never go home and hadn't the least desire to exchange his present existence for another. Hotel staff seldom spoke of their plans for the future, perhaps for fear of failing to fulfill their ambitions if they wasted too many words on them in advance. They worked and slept, worked and slept, roused from oblivion by the alarm clocks that signaled the start of each new day.

Because Erneste spoke fluent German and French as well as some English and Italian, the management used to send him down to the landing stage whenever guests or new additions to the staff were expected. At the height of the season this could often happen several times a day. Depending on the number of guests, their luggage was conveyed to the hotel in a cable car by one or two floor waiters, or, if they were busy elsewhere, by a couple of pages. Erneste's job was to deal with the guests' requests and queries. While awaiting the arrival of the cable car in which the Grand Hotel could be comfortably reached in any weather, they surveyed the scenery. They particularly admired the emerald-green lake whose pellucid waters were a temptation to swim in them all year around. This was inadvisable except in August, however, because the water was icy cold and not to be braved by any but the hardiest and most thick-skinned males. Most guests preferred to retire to the shade of the trees, where cool drinks—light white wine or assorted cocktails—were served. Now and then, when overcome with boredom, they would bestir themselves sufficiently to go for a stroll, either to the Giessbach Falls or down to the Lake of Brienz. To the lake on foot and back by cable car was worth the modicum of effort required—indeed, it was a pleasure.

On the last Sunday in May 1935 Erneste went down to the landing stage by himself. The sky was clear, but a thick layer of mist floated above the water. It was considerably colder than the day before, and had rained heavily that morning. No hotel guests were expected this Sunday. The most recent arrivals, a Russian family from Paris complete with grandmother and two servants, had checked in last night.

Erneste was waiting for the steamer. His was an unplanned existence. Any plans affecting him were made by others, people who knew their business and to whom he willingly deferred. His work at the hotel brought him more than just a sense of security; he felt snug there. Having always been alone, he was barely conscious of his solitude. At night, when he sank wearily into bed, he felt safe, and that sensation lulled him to sleep at once. He had no reason to wish for a change in his circumstances.

He could have gone on living like that for many years more. The war of which everyone spoke was a distant threat. It was still just a word, and as long as it didn't make itself felt there was no serious cause for concern.

Erneste stood beside the lake and watched the little steamer draw nearer. On the foredeck, as they gradually increased in size, he made out a trio of figures with two members of the crew—short, sturdy men in uniform—moving around in front of them. One was holding the hawser he would throw out and make fast to a bollard once he'd vaulted ashore.

Erneste was waiting for some additions to the hotel staff. The receptionist had handed him a slip of paper bearing their names and particulars: Jakob Meier, a young German trainee waiter from Cologne, and Trudi and Fanny Gerber, two Swiss girls from Sumiswald who would be employed in the hotel laundry. He glanced at his watch. The steamer was on time. It was half-past four when the vessel nudged the landing stage and jolted it.

While still on board the girls hovered behind Jakob in subdued silence, as if using the German youngster to conceal them from view. They politely murmured their names, but so softly that Erneste scarcely caught them. This was probably the first trip they'd ever made on their own, in fact they might never have left their village before. They were wearing threadbare clothes and lace gloves yellow with age. No one had told them that lace gloves were unsuitable for a laundry maid; on the contrary, some well-meaning soul had probably urged them to wear those gloves. Heaven alone knew where they'd acquired them— possibly at a rummage sale.

Jakob offered to carry the girls' suitcases. As he stooped to pick them up, flexing his knees a little because he was so tall, and looked up at Erneste from below, a lock of dark hair fell over his right eye, which was gray. His gaze was so forthright and open that Erneste had to meet it. He didn't look away but stared back. Timidly, the two girls stepped ashore with Jakob at their heels. When Erneste made his way up the narrow gangway to fetch the rest of the luggage he passed so close to the young man that they almost touched.

His emotions were unequivocal and, consequently, threatening, but he managed to concentrate on what had to be done. While the two girls stood on the landing stage, staring forlornly at the ground, he carried Jakob's luggage down the gangway, so his nervous tremor wasn't noticeable. He had never encountered anyone who seemed to hold himself so erect. The young man from Germany moved with purposeful ease, as if he had long ago made up his mind to go far in life and outshine everyone in his path. At the same time, there was something gentle and dreamy about him. He was in no hurry, for all his resolute air, and gave those around him plenty of time to observe and admire him.

And so, on the last Sunday in May 1935, Erneste found himself face to face with nineteen-year-old Jakob Meier for the first time, in the presence of two mute girls whose lips would remain sealed throughout their six months at the Grand Hotel. Trudi and Fanny merely nodded at Erneste when he bade them welcome. They seemed to have left the power of speech behind in their village across the lake.

It wasn't until all four of them were standing on the shore that Jakob shook Erneste's hand and introduced himself. "Jakob Meier," he said simply, and the handshake that accompanied this formal introduction seemed to say: "Here I am, having come here purely for your sake." The little world in which Erneste had so blithely installed himself collapsed under the aegis of Jakob Meier's sha-dow. He quit that world for evermore—for evermore, he knew it—and gladly, unresistingly left it behind. He was entering uncharted territory, and uncharted territory was what he had always longed for without realizing it. Caught in the fine mesh of Jakob's net, he felt safer there than in the infinity of ocean in which he had thoughtlessly and aimlessly been swimming until now. It was Jakob's handshake that wrought this change at a stroke, the cool, firm grip of the long, slender fingers that clasped his own.

Jakob gave him an unabashed stare. Perhaps he'd seen through him. *Had* he seen through him? Later on they would talk about everything, or almost everything, but never about that. There were subjects one didn't discuss, and the longer they knew each other the more numerous such subjects became. At that moment Erneste vowed to help the young man, to stand by him like a brother, to extricate him from any predicament, to ward off any threat, to preserve him from mortal danger even at the cost of his own life. The thoughts that ran through Erneste's head at that moment were so intense that they retained their immediacy thirty years later. He seemed to see Jakob as the son he would never have, as the sympathetic brother he'd never had, as the father and mother he would have liked, and as many other things— things he couldn't even admit to himself.

Jakob told him frankly that this was not only his first job at a regular hotel, but his first regular job of any kind. He was just nineteen, the only son of a widow, and had grown up in humble circumstances in Cologne. His father had been killed in France in 1918, shortly before the war ended. The widow jealously hoarded her late husband's letters and photos, but Jakob himself had never missed him. He hadn't seen much of the world before, but a bit more than the two girls, who were now standing huddled closely together. They didn't survey their surroundings, just stared at their feet and their suitcases and showed no sign of noticing what was going on around them.

Although Jakob hadn't seen much of the world, he'd grown up in a big city, and Erneste surmised that this had left its mark on him. He would be starting right at the bottom in Giessbach, but Erneste felt sure there was nothing to prevent his rapid promotion. His talent was obvious. Jakob gave a sudden smile, although Erneste hadn't spoken, that being the surest way of not making enemies needlessly.

While the steamer was laboriously casting off and heading away from the shore, the two of them stowed the luggage on the front bench of the cable car. The girls sat down on the rearmost bench and didn't move. Scared stiff of being spoken to by the two young men, they spent the brief trip to the hotel staring timidly, earnestly, at their glove-encased hands. They didn't look where they were going or out the window, quite unlike Jakob, who was interested in anything novel and unfamiliar. He asked Erneste questions, wanted to know when this funicular, of which a photograph appeared in *Meyers Konversationslexikon*, had been constructed. "Back in 1875," Erneste replied, and, when the Grand Hotel came into view, went on to tell Jakob the name of the man who had designed the massive building: "Horace Edouard Davinet. It was completed in 1879. Many important people have stayed here since then—princes, industrialists and big land-owners from all over Europe." He was telling him only what he told everyone, but he spoke more softly than usual. His tone was a trifle constrained.

Jakob had never ridden in a cable car before. He was interested in knowing how often it was used and whether there had ever been an accident. Erneste had heard all these questions scores of times, so he found it easy to answer them on this occasion too. He answered them gladly, happy to be able to do so in such a practiced manner, for every word that escaped the young man's lips delighted him, and he didn't mind if Jakob noticed how much pleasure he derived from the sight of him and his unfeigned, almost childlike curiosity. During the ride, which took only six or seven minutes, Jakob confided that this was his very first sight of mountains except in photographs, and that he was looking forward to his job because he hadn't done anything worth mentioning so far. He had left school early and had always dreamed of going out into the world. "And now at last I really have." Erneste smiled. "Just like me," he said. "I was like that too—I couldn't wait to conquer the world." He had found a kindred spirit.

3

The allocation of sleeping quarters wasn't one of Erneste's responsibilities, so it was pure chance that the two young men were assigned a room together. Members of staff were housed either in pairs in tiny attic rooms in the hotel itself or in dormitories in an annex. The morning after Jakob's arrival the alarm clock went off punctually at six. They were hardly out of bed before Erneste, who had slept badly, was instructing his new roommate in his duties. To begin with, these were menial tasks requiring neither intelligence nor special aptitudes, just a certain sense of tidiness and cleanliness.

It was still chilly an hour later, when Erneste handed Jakob a broom and told him to sweep all the terraces and outside steps, a job that would take him several hours, if not the whole morning. He mustn't hurry, Erneste emphasized, because it was essential that guests looking up from their breakfast or leaning over their balconies in their bathrobes be spared the sight of hectic activity. They must never get the impression that the Grand Hotel was understaffed, or that its employees were overworked and rushed off their feet. "Take it easy," Erneste told Jakob.

"Act as if you had all the time in the world. Don't work too quickly or too slowly—just work steadily, then the guests will feel at ease. Never forget, they've no wish to be reminded that there's another world outside Giessbach. Look up from your work now and then, and if you catch some guest's eye, don't look away. Smile back and nod, but don't overdo it or you'll embarrass people. Never be pushy, always self-effacing. It's presumptuous of an employee to be arrogant."

Erneste briefly checked on Jakob twice during the first two hours. He was making good progress. At ten o'clock he asked him to come with him. "You must be hungry, aren't you? Everyone gets hungry around this time." Jakob nodded. He propped his broom against the wall and followed Erneste into the hotel by a rear entrance. They made their way through the kitchen, where lunch was being prepared—a hive of activity in which the chefs' raucous voices drowned all other sounds. Other members of staff were flocking to the canteen behind and ahead of them, some coming the other way. The passage was narrow, and people trying to squeeze past each other were thrust against the walls, which were damp in places.

In the canteen they had some coffee and hurriedly wolfed the guests' breakfast leftovers: rolls and croissants, butter and preserves, ham and cheese—anything that had been laid out on two long tables. They wouldn't get their midday meal until the last guests had left the dining room, which could often be after three, so it was advisable to stock up for the next few strenuous hours.

For a short time the canteen, too, was a scene of hectic activity that differed from the display of calm composure to which the management attached such importance when guests were around. This turmoil recurred at the same time every morning, between ten and half-past.

Erneste went on ahead and pointed to two vacant places. They sat down side by side at one of the pair of wooden tables that took up most of the room. The canteen made a gloomy impression. The only window, which was covered by a faded blind, was small and dirty and wholly superfluous. The bench on which they sat had no back to it.

Erneste introduced Jakob to the colleagues nearest them and the latecomers who took their places when the others had gotten up and hurried off, but Jakob felt convinced that none of them registered his name any more than he registered theirs. Too many people were coming and going, there was too much noise, and since most of the names sounded foreign he would have failed to memorize them even under more favorable conditions. Besides, many of them seemed to be deep in thought despite the noise. Some simply ignored him, others pulled faces as if they didn't grasp what Erneste was getting at. Jakob had never seen so many different nationalities in one place, not even at the central station in Cologne. While his left elbow was brushing that of an Italian, a Serbian's hand patted his shoulder, and while he was nodding to a Spaniard, a Portuguese turned to go. All were impatient, none looked him in the eye.

None of the staff who entered and left the canteen during this short break for breakfast was older than thirty-five, the majority being between sixteen and twenty-five. Senior hotel employees seldom quit their places of work at this hour. Moreover, the people who congregated here were exclusively male because the chambermaids were busy cleaning the rooms.

Although it didn't escape Erneste that the young German was attracting no more attention than any other trainee, it filled him with pride to be sitting beside Jakob as a matter of course. The others obviously didn't share his admiration. He searched their faces for a glimmer of envy and found none—not yet, but a second look at Jakob would soon change their minds. Jakob was handsome, as they couldn't fail to notice in the long run. He, at least, was not unaffected by Jakob's ease of manner. The others might be familiar with the feeling of friendship between men, but the feeling that linked him and this youngster was something quite else—that they couldn't know. He almost grasped Jakob's hand and squeezed it, but he naturally refrained from doing so. For one thing, he feared he might be rebuffed; for another, he was well aware how unseemly such overt gestures were, even here, where the rules weren't as strict as they were outside.

Erneste was in a position to help his new-found friend. He showed him everything a waiter had to know, and while tutoring Jakob he could watch him, unobtrusively at first but later with somewhat fewer inhibitions. He felt as if he wanted to slip inside him, and before long he didn't care if Jakob noticed this. One thing was certain: he would make a perfect waiter of him.

Erneste taught him all the rules of etiquette and showed him what a perfect waiter must be able to do—a time-consuming process entailing correction and encouragement. It soon dawned on him that Jakob had absolutely no objection to being watched as he cleaned and polished shoes, folded napkins and table-cloths. Jakob didn't take offense at this. He soon seemed to grasp that Erneste had no wish to bully him, only to supervise and look at him: supervise him like a child, look at him like a picture. Although it was an illicit desire that drove Erneste to do this, Jakob didn't appear to find his scrutiny irksome or embarrassing, from which he inferred that the boy was used to being stared at by his fellow mortals. All that surprised him was that Jakob wasn't the cynosure of every eye. Erneste wasn't jealous. On the contrary, he didn't mind sharing the sight of his protégé with other people. Jakob, he felt, was entitled to be admired and loved and stared at. His way of moving, speaking, and daydreaming—to Erneste, everything about him seemed utterly superlative. There was nothing to prevent him from becoming a perfect waiter.

———————

After only two weeks, during which Jakob—to cite only some of his numerous occupations—had acted as an errand boy, gardener's assistant, car washer, bootblack and porter, Erneste persuaded Monsieur Flamin, the *maître sommelier*, to permit him to make himself useful in the dining room—a job appropriate to his talents at last. This was an exceptional honor, for trainees weren't usually allowed anywhere near guests at mealtimes until they'd spent several months performing the humblest tasks. Jakob himself bore some responsibility for Erneste's successful intervention, having several times urged him at night, before they went to bed, to speak to Flamin on his behalf. He was getting bored outside, he said—he wanted to be near some guests, so Erneste had no choice but to tackle Flamin, who never regretted having given his assent. Jakob proved to be a quick learner.

He began by working in the background, immediately next to the serving table against the wall, where it was never very light. There he lent a helping hand whenever requested to do so by Monsieur Flamin, Erneste and the other waiters. Every one of his superiors was entitled to call on his services at any time and for the most trivial reason.

While carrying out his allotted tasks, Jakob never took his eyes off the others, neither Monsieur Flamin, the *maître sommelier*, nor the *garçons*, nor the *chefs de rang*. Their relative seniority was less apparent from their style of dress than from the speed at which they moved. The faster they bustled from table to table, the more junior their status within the hierarchy. But every status was important in its own way. The more measured someone's tread, the more important he was, the more obvious his assimilation of the guests' ways, and the more familiar with them he could afford to be, though any form of familiarity had to remain within permissible bounds. Most familiar with them of all, of course, was the hotel manager, Herr Direktor Emil Wagner, who often failed to show his face for days on end. It was better to be prepared for him to reappear at any moment, however, because he came down like a ton of bricks on anyone he caught misbehaving. Herr Wagner stood no nonsense, nor could you expect him to pardon you in a hurry. He was a vindictive man with a violent temper, though he never displayed it in front of guests.

Jakob was filled with admiration for the elegance and facility with which the waiters avoided the obstacles in their path. He marveled at their deftness and poise as they made their way across the dining room with loaded trays on their shoulders, simultaneously keeping an eye on the tables in their care and watching out for signals from their superiors. According to Erneste, indecision was a characteristic mainly of female diners, who often revoked their choices in favor of others, only to revoke those a moment later. It was inappropriate to comment on this in any way, Erneste emphasized. Their right to freedom of choice and indecision had to be greeted with an air of understanding. That was as much a waiter's professional attribute as immaculate fingernails and clean socks.

Jakob started at the very bottom, as a *commis de rang*. He filled the heavy crystal carafes with Seltzer water, lighted the candles in the candelabra and plate warmers, and polished the knives, forks and spoons. Meantime, he had an opportunity to study the waiters both at close range and from afar, noting their every movement, every facial expression and flick of the wrist. After only a few days he felt capable of emulating them and itched to do so. He said as much to Erneste, but it was a while before he was allowed near an occupied table.

He spent three weeks performing his lowly tasks in the big dining room, which contained some twenty-five tables of various sizes. Not only did he perform them to Monsieur Flamin's entire satisfaction, but no complaints were heard from any other quarter. He silently disposed of anything deposited on the serving table, whether used napkins, brimming ashtrays, snapped toothpicks, or dirty plates and glasses.

One night he was privileged to be personally introduced to Herr Direktor Wagner. The manager gave him a benevolent smile, patted him on the shoulder, said, "Good work, my boy," and walked on. Jakob didn't see him again for days, but he learned the same night why Wagner showed his face so seldom, unlike his wife: he suffered from violent bouts of depression. When overcome by one of these fits of melancholia he would closet himself in his darkened office for days on end, incommunicado to anyone but his wife. He slept in his clothes, didn't wash, and had to be coaxed to eat.

Jakob knew that a *commis de rang* could speak above a murmur only when directly addressed by guests and in the absence of any senior waiter who could have hurried to their aid, for instance when they inquired the way to the cloakroom—by which, of course, they meant not the cloakroom but the facility situated beyond it, namely, the *toilettes*. For a waiter to indicate the way to the *toilettes* by pointing, let alone jerking his chin in their direction, would warrant his dismissal if the manager spotted him. Consequently, everyone strove to observe the correct etiquette. None of the Grand Hotel's employees found this difficult, for uncouth individuals did not apply for jobs as waiters; they became butchers or bricklayers.

Jakob also learned that it was extremely impolite for waiters of any rank to converse together in the presence of guests. Such conversations were permissible only when one waiter's inability to answer a guest's inquiry rendered it essential for him to consult another. Jakob acquired many tips of this kind during the next few weeks, not only thanks to Erneste but from personal experience, by closely observing various situations of a similar nature. As Erneste had grasped the very first day, Jakob was alert, adaptable and coolheaded. He got everything right the first time and appeared to see and hear all that mattered without ever giving the impression that he was watching and listening from curiosity alone. He never seemed indiscreet, absorbed and assimilated all he saw, and did not forget a thing once he had learned it. Like any efficient waiter, he soon conveyed the feeling that he had no personal interest in what was going on around him but was solely intent on doing right by the guests, which also meant treating them with complete impartiality.

———•◦•———

On the morning of Jakob's second day at work, Erneste accompanied him to the tailoring department, which was housed in the former spa hotel that had closed around the turn of the century. This rather dilapidated building, which was situated a few hundred yards from the hotel and could not be seen from there, also accommodated the short-term seasonal workers, the linen store, and the clothing store. The latter contained all the various garments which, having been unpicked and restitched again and again, had clothed and would continue to clothe generations of waiters and chambermaids. While they came and went in quick succession, the aprons and blouses, trousers and jackets on the shelves and hangers calmly awaited their resuscitation by the lithe young bodies that would replenish them with flesh and life for varying periods.

The person in charge of the clothing store was Frau Adamowicz from Geneva, who also ran the hotel's tailoring department. Polish by birth, brought up in Switzerland, and trained as a *couturière* in Paris, she presided over her realm of slumbering garments as prudently and incorruptibly as she did over the three needlewomen who, with bowed heads and nimble fingers, toiled in her service from early in the morning until late at night. She never took her eyes off them, and despite her cool manner, which might have been only a veneer, she loved them like an elder sister immune from all criticism. They were delighted when words of praise escaped her lips but didn't expect them, and they humbly accepted her reproofs but weren't surprised by them, knowing that they were constantly in her thoughts because she disliked thinking of herself—if she ever did so. Her only child was said to have died in infancy, but she never alluded to it. Rumors were all that was known.

That Frau Adamowicz's minions did a good job was plain to see. The three women, of whom the eldest had been employed at Giessbach for nineteen years, repaired napkins and tablecloths, bedspreads and sheets day after day. They also tailored garments for new employees in accordance with Frau Adamowicz's instructions. If she was out the new employees would be sent away and told to come back later, because she alone was entitled to take their measurements. She also submitted every napkin and tablecloth, sheet and bedspread to personal inspection before handing it over to be repaired, or, if it was no longer fit for guests, weeded it out and tossed it onto the cleaning-rag pile after tearing it into strips with her own hands.

Erneste and Jakob entered the tailoring department at a quarter past ten, after a late breakfast. Frau Adamowicz's minions were seated at their work, one of the four sewing machines was in use, and the room smelled of glowing coals and dried flowers. The three women looked up and smiled without speaking. Frau Adamowicz, who was bound to have heard the men come in, would appear before long.

She emerged from the clothing store, almost simultaneously removing her glasses and putting them in her apron pocket. The ends of the tape measure around her neck reposed on her bosom, and a pincushion worn like a bracelet jutted menacingly from her left wrist. Her appearance in the sewing room was preceded by an unaccountable stir, as if she were propelling the air along in front of her.

Erneste introduced Jakob to the four women. He had scarcely uttered Jakob's name when Frau Adamowicz repeated it: "Jakob? Meier?" She replaced her glasses, went over to her cutting table and proceeded to leaf through a bulky ledger, starting at the back. Having found a blank page, she wrote something on it, then looked up and surveyed Jakob from head to foot. "Now we'll take your measurements," she said, pulling the tape measure from around her neck. "Kindly remove your jacket. Stand up straight, please don't shuffle from foot to foot, and keep your head up." Her French was so clearly enunciated that even Jakob could understand it in spite of her Polish accent.

While she was preparing to take his measurements, Erneste sat down beside the window, where he could watch the three needlewomen as well as Jakob and Frau Adamowicz. One of them rose and went over to the cutting table, picked up a pencil and bent over the ledger.

Although physical contact with Jakob was an unavoidable part of the measuring process, Frau Adamowicz went about her work in a characteristically easy, experienced manner. Without any misplaced shyness, she did whatever she had to do to give the new trainee waiter a spruce appearance. Erneste, seated on his chair, found it easy to put himself in her place. He watched her without blushing, following her practiced, authoritative movements with rapt attention. He stared spellbound at the slowly moving image, his eyes tracing the course of her hands as they traveled across Jakob's body. No one asked why he didn't leave the room. None of the others did.

Frau Adamowicz started at the top. She encircled Jakob's neck with the tape measure and tightened it until there was room between it and his throat for her forefinger, nothing more. Her assistant noted down the collar size in the employees' measurement book.

Frau Adamowicz's instructions were unmistakable, although she didn't speak particularly loudly. "Spread your arms," she said, and Jakob promptly did as he was told: he stretched out his arms at right angles to his body. Little patches of sweat had formed under his armpits. As he spread his arms, the cuffs of his soft shirt rode up and exposed his wrists. One of the needlewomen looked up. The one who was taking down the measurements stared intently at the ledger and waited. Her forefinger exerted so much pressure on the pencil that the lead snapped.

When Frau Adamowicz came to measure Jakob's chest, he involuntarily deflated it a little. "No, don't," she said. It seemed she'd been expecting him to do just that because everyone reacted in the same way. "Stand up straight, absolutely straight, and look straight ahead," was all she said, and Jakob resumed his upright stance. She stood on tiptoe and leaned forward a little, put the tape measure around his chest, and tightened it over his breastbone. "Breathe in. Now breathe out." Her assistant, who had meantime sharpened the pencil, jotted down two figures under the heading "Chest Measurement". The two women seemed to be trying to outdo each other in conscientiousness.

"That was for shirts, vests, and jackets." Frau Adamowicz probably said that to every candidate at this stage of the proceedings. If so, each of her three assistants must have been expecting to hear the words at precisely that juncture. She had said the same thing to Erneste, too, when he first arrived. Next, she applied one end of the tape measure to Jakob's left shoulder and measured the length of his left arm, first to the elbow, then to the wrist, first extended, then bent. After that she measured his right arm in the same way. No two arms are identical, Erneste reflected, and Jakob was probably thinking the same at that very moment.

Jakob's armpit hair felt silky. It was moist and somewhat fairer than the hair on his head. Erneste couldn't see it now, but he had seen it that morning, while Jakob was washing. He was sitting twenty feet away, but he could distinctly feel it on the back of his hand.

Before going down on her knees, Frau Adamowicz stooped and put the tape measure around Jakob's waist, hips and buttocks. She called out a series of measurements, which were noted down and, on one occasion, erased and rewritten in short order. "Spread your legs a little," she said, and Jakob's rubber soles squeaked as he complied. A moment later he was standing there with his legs apart, just as she wanted—but not too far apart, because he froze when she abruptly called, "Stop!"

The two men's eyes met as Frau Adamowicz applied the tape measure to the inside of Jakob's left thigh, exerting gentle pressure on it with her thumb. She ran the tape down to his knee, then to his ankle, called out a figure and then, to be on the safe side, repeated the process in two stages, from the top of the thigh to the knee and from there to the ankle. She shifted her weight onto the other knee and turned to the left slightly in order to measure Jakob's right inside leg. Erneste, still holding his gaze over the top of her head, flushed suddenly. Jakob lowered his eyes: he had understood. Frau Adamowicz straightened up, and the blood slowly receded from Erneste's cheeks. What had Jakob grasped that he hadn't known already?

Frau Adamowicz had now taken all his measurements, but he wouldn't, of course, get a tailor-made suit. None of the Grand Hotel's employees got tailor-made suits, nor would any of them have dreamed of expecting one; you contented yourself with what you were given. Four efficient women were at work here, so you could rely on their producing a good job—one in which you would look presentable. Only senior employees who had seen something of the world possessed suits of their own, for instance Monsieur Flamin and the *chef de réception*, who had worked in Cairo, Paris, and London.

Frau Adamowicz turned and disappeared into the clothing store, from which she soon emerged bearing one of the waiter's outfits customarily worn at Giessbach's Grand Hotel: black tails, vest, and shirt with a starched dickey. The system that prevailed in the clothing store enabled Frau Adamowicz, who never allowed things to get out of hand, to locate them quickly. She hung the garments in Jakob's size over a chair and stepped back. The assistant who had entered Jakob's measurements in the ledger had returned to her place and was removing pins from the hem of a chambermaid's dress draped over her knees and trailing on the floor.

———•—•———

Frau Adamowicz asked Jakob to try the things on, so he started to undress. She turned away and her three assistants concentrated on their work. Erneste and Jakob might almost have been alone in the room. Jakob continued to undress while Erneste looked on. Frau Adamowicz, who had discreetly turned her back, was facing in Erneste's direction, but he refused to be deterred by her gaze. What, after all, could she see, other than one young man watching another just as he might have watched himself undressing in a mirror? However talented she might be at putting herself in another person's place, she couldn't read his thoughts. His face was expressionless.

Jakob unbuttoned his shirt, took it off, and tossed it onto a chair. He was wearing an undershirt, darned in several places, the sleeves of which came down to his elbows. He stooped to undo his shoelaces, removed his black shoes and put them under the chair that was serving him as a clothes rack. He smoothed his hair down with his right hand as he straightened up, and the sleeve of his undershirt rode up far enough to expose his upper arm. It was slender but muscular, even though he wasn't accustomed to manual labor. He unbuckled his belt and undid his fly buttons. He pulled the belt out of his waistband with a snap, then pulled his trousers down over his buttocks and thighs with both hands, raised his right leg, bent forward, gripped his right trouser leg by the cuff and slid it over his calf, ankle, and foot. He climbed out of the other trouser leg in just the same way—just as Erneste himself would have done. Any man would have done the same in Jakob's situation. It was the most natural series of movements in the world, but to Erneste it was something special.

Jakob was quite unembarrassed. Erneste found this remarkable, because he was naturally entitled, if not duty-bound, to display at least a hint of embarrassment. But he didn't seem to mind being watched while undressing. Erneste sat there without moving, anxious not to miss a single phase of the process. Jakob was still holding his belt, which dangled against his leg and brushed the floor. He wound it around his right hand and deposited it on the chair, where the leather coil loosened a little like a spring unwinding.

Jakob looked good in his underwear. Erneste almost wished the four women could see his friend as he was now, as he himself was seeing him, but they didn't look up and continued to concentrate on their work. They must surely have been under instructions not to embarrass the men who came to try on clothes by watching them. Erneste counted himself lucky to be a man. Being a man, he could watch.

He went over to help Jakob try on his waiter's outfit. He handed him the trousers, but Jakob wanted the shirt first. Erneste took it from the chair and unfolded it. Since Jakob made no move to take the garment, Erneste unbuttoned it for him and went around the back to help him on with it. Jakob, who was slightly taller than Erneste, stooped and bent his left arm behind him. He missed the sleeve opening, so Erneste grasped his wrist. Jakob didn't recoil at his touch. His skin was cool and firm, smooth and hairless. Trembling a little, Erneste guided Jakob's left arm into the sleeve. Then he did the same with the right arm. This time Jakob made no attempt to find the opening. He left it up to Erneste, submitted to his guidance, bent his arm behind him and waited for Erneste to grasp it. Erneste did so. He tightened his grip on Jakob's wrist and guided it into the sleeve. The hand did not pull away, it tensed. It was the hand of a man, a resolute man.

While Jakob was buttoning up the shirt, which smelled faintly of starch, Erneste smoothed it down for him. As he patted it down over his shoulders and back with both hands, he could feel what lay beneath them: little protrusions and hollows, shoulders, shoulder blades and armpits, alternations of firm and soft. But he could sense that Frau Adamowicz was growing impatient. One last touch, and he detached himself from Jakob's shadow and came and stood in front of him, passing him the trousers, belt and vest in turn. He stood in front of Jakob, only inches from him, and watched his legs disappear into the black trousers at close range, and while Jakob was buttoning them up he looked into Erneste's eyes, and when he smiled Erneste knew that he was lost: that he had gained something and forfeited it at the same time—that the profit he had made would be his loss. He had a strange presentiment, a vague sense of something incomprehensible, something that lurked behind his excitement as if concealed by a bright façade and was trying to signal its presence by means of unintelligible signs; something foolish and distressing, some threat he wanted no part of, some foolish, distressing threat that lay behind the happiness and joy that surged through him. Erneste couldn't swim, but he wouldn't have drowned had he jumped into the lake at that moment; he would have swum far out, unafraid of failing to reach the opposite shore. But he also knew that he would be happy only while Jakob was happy too, and that he must make him happy to preserve his own happiness. He had captured Jakob's attention—succeeded in doing what he hadn't dared to hope for. He didn't possess Jakob yet; he was obsessed with him.

But time was passing and they had to be quick. Erneste continued to stand beside Jakob until he was fully dressed. Then he took two paces to the rear. The tails were an almost perfect fit. Frau Adamowicz, who had turned around by this time, took a piece of tailor's chalk and marked the minor alterations to be made to the trousers. "Germans are always the tallest," she said, and Jakob grinned. "Yes," Erneste said with a proud smile, "you're right."

4

On October 5, 1966, three weeks after Jakob's first letter, almost to the day, Erneste received some more mail from the States, same sender, same address. Unlike the first letter, however, this one left no room for hope. It merely confirmed Erneste's worst fears. He had counted on getting another letter, it was true, but he hadn't expected it so soon. Jakob was hurrying him along.

Although he'd secretly hoped that the problem would go away if only he ignored it, closer inspection proved that it had always existed. It wasn't going away; it was too palpable to be brushed aside. His abiding nightmare, the one from which he never awoke, featured a high wall—one he could neither clear nor skirt around.

Nobody asked why he was looking so overtired. People always practiced restraint where Erneste was concerned, deterred from coming too close by his aura of dignified gentility. His colleagues at the Restaurant am Berg left him in peace, and he never saw anyone else during the day.

He had put Jakob's first letter away somewhere, hoping that it would get mislaid. No matter where it was, however, Erneste could never have brought himself to destroy it. He waited. Although he had been expecting another letter, he winced when he found it in his mailbox. There was nothing he could have told Jakob, so he hadn't written to him. But Jakob obviously had no time to lose. He didn't trust him. He thought him capable of failing to reply, and he was right.

So Jakob had written again, and if he didn't write back, more letters were bound to follow. Jakob was in a bad way. He was in a hurry because his problem brooked no delay, so he was pestering Erneste. Having taken it into his head to obtain something, he was forcing the pace. Jakob's future, his wellbeing in America, was at stake. Jakob himself was at stake.

Erneste felt cornered. What he had wrapped up and stowed away in the corner of his mind was threatening to reappear, as fresh and potent as ever. It hadn't been wrapped up carefully enough, and the pain was unendurable. Possibly unaware of his cruelty, Jakob had ripped the parcel open at a stroke. If you don't open it, he was saying, I'll open it for you, and its effect was as potent as a snakebite. Its venom had reached Erneste from thousands of miles away. A letter. Letter after letter from New York addressed to him, who very seldom left Switzerland. His memories of Giessbach, which he had believed buried by Jakob's persistent silence since the end of the war, were still alive. The passing years had not impaired the clarity of those memories. His wounds hadn't healed; they were open and smarting.

The letter he found reposing in his mailbox on October 5, 1966, sandwiched between a leaflet advertising cheap flights to Paris and London and the local weekly giveaway, had been posted in New York a week earlier, on September 29. Like the first letter, this one had been airmailed. The thin envelope was pale blue in color, the postmark crisply impressed.

Erneste did not possess a telephone, although he might sometimes have felt tempted to check the weather forecast, the latest news, or the time. But whom should he have called? He had no friends, maintained no personal contact with his colleagues at work, and had nothing to say to his fleeting acquaintances except on the rare occasions when he sought their company. He couldn't recall their voices or what they looked like. Once out of sight, each was indistinguishable from the next. His cousin in Paris? Yes, he'd like to have spoken with Julie, but foreign calls were expensive. Discounting Christmas or New Year's, they wouldn't have called each other very often. A telephone was a luxury.

Had he possessed a telephone, Jakob would have discovered his number. Jakob wasn't just sitting there waiting. Having found out Erneste's address, he certainly wouldn't have found it hard to discover his phone number. Had he possessed a telephone, Jakob would have called him long ago. His future was at stake, so saving on phone bills was beside the point. Would the consonants and vowels that assailed Erneste's ear have combined at once into an unmistakably familiar voice?

Would he have recognized it? No, Jakob's voice was unfamiliar to him. He wouldn't have recognized it because, if there was one thing he couldn't recall, it was Jakob's voice. It had utterly slipped his mind. All that he ever heard, and only very rarely, was a whisper in his ear. A faint whisper, and whenever he heard it he gave a start and looked around.

Erneste's considerations differed from Jakob's, that much was certain. Over in America, Jakob obviously didn't think it necessary to put himself in Erneste's shoes. He might be in despair but he wasn't devoid of courage, and he didn't show it even if he was. He would get his way. Even if his wishes weren't met in the end, he would have done his utmost to fulfill them. There was always a way out, and to find it he now needed Erneste just as he had needed him in Giessbach, as he had later needed Klinger, and as he had doubtless needed other people in America. Anyone who helped Jakob was entitled to a few moments of his attention and, with a little bit of luck, to his commendation; anyone unable to help him was dismissed without another thought. Jakob was indomitable, he'd allowed for everything. He was giving Erneste no peace, no time to think.

He'd managed to discover Erneste's address. Having discovered it, he knew that Erneste was still alive, and since Erneste was still alive he could be useful to him. Erneste could approach Klinger on his behalf. He would find some way of helping him out of his predicament, some way of wheedling money out of Klinger, and Klinger, for old time's sake, would surely do all that was necessary. That was how Jakob had figured it out, and he was probably right. Erneste and Klinger would help him for old time's sake, each after his own fashion. Erneste would play the role he'd always played: that of the scout and trail-blazer. His task was to jog an old man's memory and extract some money from him. His task was to plead Jakob's case with the celebrated Julius Klinger, whom he scarcely knew and who would not, of course, remember him because in those days, like Erneste himself, the great author had had eyes for Jakob alone. Klinger was a globe-trotter who had changed continents as often as other men change their shirts. He had stayed at so many hotels and known so many prominent people, he certainly wouldn't remember a waiter he'd last seen thirty years ago.

Why hadn't Jakob written to Klinger himself? Why did he need a go-between? Was he too embarrassed to solicit Klinger's help direct? Was he afraid of being rejected, and if so why? Klinger possessed a telephone. A world-famous, sought-after man like him must have a telephone, so why hadn't Jakob simply called him? The celebrated author's number was in the book, Erneste had already checked. It was easy enough to find, but Jakob evidently hadn't called him. Was Klinger refusing to speak with him? Had he dropped Jakob the way Jakob dropped other people? Long engrossed in thoughts of Jakob, Erneste still hadn't opened the letter. There was no avoiding it.

Erneste was awaiting the arrival of his cousin Julie. She was the only person he could have discussed Jakob's letters with, the only person who could have advised him—not that he would ask her to. That was unthinkable. The understanding that prevailed between them was based on discretion. Her interest in his personal affairs was only slight.

Julie was coming on her own. She had paid an annual visit to Switzerland for the past twenty years, and for the past twenty years her husband the toy manufacturer had stayed behind in Paris. Their children had already left home. On the pretext of taking the waters for her arthritis, she ostensibly paid an annual visit to Zurzach, where she had actually been only once in order to bone up on the local scenery and the spa facilities. This was in case she was questioned about the place at home, although her husband, who probably didn't even know what the waters at Zurzach were good for, was as uninterested in the scenery there as he was in his wife's state of health. Meanwhile, Julie had for years checked into a small hotel not far from Erneste's apartment, there to meet with her longtime English lover. Her unwitting husband allowed her to go without ever smelling a rat. She hardly ever mentioned him to Erneste.

When Julie and Erneste wanted to talk in private they did so at Erneste's apartment or at a café in the town center. Sunday being Erneste's only day off, their meetings were few and far between, but although they saw each other so seldom, the intimacy between them remained intact no matter how long it was since their last meeting. Julie discussed things with Erneste she couldn't have mentioned at home, even to her best woman friend, whereas Erneste's affairs were never touched on by either of them. Erneste was content with the role of listener and, since Julie talked a lot, that role had assumed growing importance as the years went by.

Erneste was fond of his garrulous cousin because he could trust her without having to confide in her. Being one who lived a lie, she took no exception to his own way of life, perhaps because her own was not entirely irreproachable. She condoned his proclivity by simply ignoring it.

Julie never tired of discussing the clandestine aspects of her life and all its resulting complications, whereas Erneste contented himself with her obvious endeavor to tolerate his true existence by disregarding it. That was her contribution. It seemed unnecessary to him to broach the subject itself. In any case, there had been nothing to tell since Jakob's departure for America.

While Julie was talking Erneste could remain silent, and his silence absolved her from giving any thought to matters that concerned him—matters she might have found disagreeable had he actually come to speak of them. She had as little wish to embarrass him as he had to embarrass her. This reinforced the bond between them, which had nothing, absolutely nothing, to do with their family ties. Those, they felt, were quite fortuitous.

Erneste enjoyed Julie's annual visits and her fondness for talking about her life, which differed so much from his. He knew that she respected him, which was more than he was entitled to expect from any other person, although her acceptance of his proclivity might only have been the price she paid for his discretion. He never reproached her and was never shocked. It didn't matter to him whom she met and whom she deceived. She tended to fancy herself the heroine of a grand romance in which Erneste, as he knew full well, played only a walk-on part.

Julie was like a sister to him. She loved him like an elder brother who had secrets but was reluctant to share them with his kid sister. He didn't want to burden her unnecessarily. She was far fonder of him than of her husband, yet a certain strangeness persisted between them. They were like two conspirators devoid of a common enemy. They might not have existed at all outside their rare meetings, not even when they sat together in the café drinking coffee, eating pastries, and eying the same men.

Julie's indulgence or indifference seemed convincing enough to be genuine. She had no idea how Erneste really lived and no wish to hear any details. She probably guessed that his life was monotonous. In the old days at Giessbach he had staked all he possessed, and everything had come easy to him. Living in Giessbach was like living on an island: what one person did was of no concern to anyone else. There he had believed he was truly alive, alive in every fiber of his body and soul.

Erneste removed Jakob's letter and the advertising leaflet from his mailbox. It was no accident, but attributable solely to the nature of the leaflet, that he had a sudden crystal-clear vision of Jakob outlined against a big white airliner, a white airliner with a white cross on its red tail fin. He was standing at the top of the gangway, looking straight ahead without seeming to notice Erneste. He was wearing a white shirt, a dark-red necktie, a pale-blue jacket, and gray slacks with a pale patch at knee height. He was slim, having scarcely aged at all—in fact he had only just reached adulthood. He laughed as he came down the steps, and all was just as it had been in the old days. His eyes were gray, his hair as dark as ever. The passage of time seemed to have been effaced, and so had the rancorous thoughts and feelings of which Erneste had been unable to divest himself for thirty years.

Jakob hadn't changed, nor had anything else. The love that filled Erneste was unaltered. His cheeks burned, his eyes brimmed with tears. It was nine o'clock, and he was standing beside his mailbox in the hallway. He was on duty in an hour's time, he had to go to work, mustn't stand there thinking. A middle-aged man fighting back his tears in the hallway—a melancholy figure.

He still couldn't shake off his waking dream. Jakob was walking casually toward him as if nothing had happened. He emerged from the shadow of the airliner's fuselage and looked in all directions, but still he didn't see him, and Erneste hadn't the strength or courage to attract his attention. Although Jakob looked through him as if he were thin air, Jakob himself remained the solid, magnetic object he always had been. Now that Erneste could see him as distinctly as if he were really there, he knew he could refuse him nothing. Whatever Jakob wanted, Erneste wanted for him, even if it was to his own detriment. Not a day had gone by since Giessbach—not one. He hadn't rid himself of Jakob, who existed and held him captive. Jakob didn't see him, yet Erneste had eyes for him alone. The image vanished after a few seconds. Jakob was fifty, he himself fifty-two. A shadow flitted past him in the hallway. Later he wondered if he'd passed someone on the stairs. All he could remember was a shadow, but perhaps it had been his own.

Erneste continued to stand in front of his mailbox and stare at the advertising leaflet, which he was holding in his right hand: an airliner above the clouds on a white background. He picked up Jakob's letter. Although it didn't burn his hand, the threat inherent in it was undiminished. He put it in his trouser pocket and shut the mailbox.

He was as incapable of shutting his eyes to this letter as he had been to the first, but this time he wouldn't wait three days before reading it. He had a pretty fair idea of what lay in store for him. He clung to the banisters, for every step that led to his apartment brought him nearer the real Jakob. Had he not opened the first letter, it would be unnecessary to open this one, but if he didn't open this one and then do as Jakob asked, the next letter wouldn't be long in coming. A week, two weeks? It might be already on its way.

Jakob, who knew him better than he knew himself, should have found it easy to make friends in New York. Was he as short of friends there as Erneste was here? How vast New York must be, and what a tiny speck in it Jakob must represent, for him to have turned to him, Erneste, for help. Jakob could have told him about this, but he had written only of his immediate concerns and would surely do the same in this second letter—not what sort of life he led, nothing about New York or the people he knew that lived there. The patrons of the Restaurant am Berg included businessmen who had visited New York. Erneste could have asked them about it, but he would never, of course, be so presumptuous as to ask them questions of a personal nature. He never asked personal questions even of his few acquaintances. There was no objection to asking questions anyone could answer without having to make personal disclosures, but what form should those questions take?

Klinger was familiar with New York, he'd lived there. Klinger was widely traveled and Jakob had accompanied him there. He could ask him about it, but he wouldn't dare. Still, he would have no choice but to pay Klinger a visit in the end, he knew it, and Klinger might already be aware of his reason for coming. Erneste had never read any of his novels, he didn't read books. Books didn't interest him. He was tired when he came home at night. If he'd opened a book instead of going to bed, he would have fallen asleep over it in no time. He'd have liked to own a TV but couldn't afford one. He was saving up. Another two years, and he would be able to buy himself one.

He didn't know much about Klinger, but he'd heard a few months ago that his wife had died. Years earlier he'd read that Klinger had declined to return to Germany in spite of numerous appeals from German politicians. Erneste, who never bought a newspaper or magazine, had read this at the hairdresser's he visited every three weeks. All the newspapers had reported Klinger's refusal, even the *Schweizer Illustrierte*, which was Erneste's usual reading matter at the salon.

According to the *Schweizer Illustrierte*, Klinger had replied that he intended to remain in Switzerland. He saw no reason to return to the native land that had driven him out. Switzerland was his new home, he declared, and he had owned a Swiss passport for several years. "One more Swiss, one less German!" quipped the hairdresser, who had read no more of Klinger's books than Erneste. These days, nobody asked Klinger to return to Germany anymore. Times had changed and he was old. He no longer commented on political developments, Erneste surmised.

He had seen Klinger once around ten years ago. He'd been sitting in the Restaurant am Berg with his wife and a stranger. Erneste had waited on him, but the great man naturally hadn't recognized him. "An imposing figure in an immaculately cut dark suit," was the manager's description of him. Many of the restaurant's customers could be described as imposing figures, notably the conductors who often ate and drank there after concerts. But equally imposing were the Swedish and German, Spanish and Italian opera singers of both sexes.

5

Erneste hadn't been expecting it. While they were walking down to the lake—it was on a Sunday morning in July, two months almost to the day after his arrival in Giessbach—Jakob had, out of the blue, draped his left arm around Erneste's shoulders and kissed him.

Nothing had happened to warrant that kiss, other than the fact that it might not have escaped Jakob how ardently Erneste had been yearning for his touch throughout those past few weeks. Sympathy for the exigencies of a man in love, especially a man in love with another man, was no reason for kissing him like that—kissing him not in the seclusion of their attic room but outside in the open and visible from all directions, a thoroughly dangerous environment in which unwelcome onlookers could be expected to appear at any moment.

Jakob didn't kiss Erneste like a brother, or like someone kissing his father or mother. He kissed him like a lover, without fear or inhibition—a trifle clumsily, too, because he probably hadn't had much practice at it. In kissing Erneste he was doing something forbidden. He knew it, yet he did it. He did it in a place where they might have been caught unawares, for hotel guests could have come upon them at any moment. The weather was fine, just the weather for strolling down to the lake—before or after a swim, with or without children, hand in hand or walking decorously apart—and returning to the hotel by cable car. They risked being seen because the shrubs and trees around them provided only sparse protection from unwelcome eyes. Jakob was endangering himself and endangering Erneste, but he overrode all his misgivings.

He wasn't deterred in the least by his own audacity. His desire to kiss his friend was evidently stronger than his fear of being rejected. In spite of his own desire for physical contact with Jakob, or for that very reason, Erneste would never so much as have ventured to brush against him, whereas Jakob, the inexperienced young man from Germany, was doing, and doing with complete unconcern, what Erneste would never have dared to do and would always be grateful for. Jakob had no fear of being rejected, so he made the first move. Wherever that move would lead in the end, it now led straight to paradise.

Jakob's tongue took possession of Erneste's mouth, invading it unimpeded. Needless to say, Erneste returned the kiss as willingly and ardently as he had received it. His breathing quickened, sucking air from Jakob's lungs, and his heart pounded. Nothing could have surprised him more than this reckless onslaught, just as nothing could have delighted him more than this fulfillment of his dearest wish. He had never dared to hope that it could genuinely be fulfilled. He had too often dreamed that Jakob's arms were around him, and now they really were. He was in paradise at last, filled with lust and sensuality, apprehension and fear of discovery.

At first, however, he strove to maintain a certain distance between them, not wanting Jakob to feel how crudely his desire was manifesting itself. Aroused as never before, with his penis engorged to bursting point, he naturally had to maintain this gap of a few inches, this hurdle, only until it was cleared by Jakob himself. When his body abruptly thrust itself against Erneste's, it was obvious that each of them was as aroused as the other. Their bodies and temperaments complemented each other.

So there they stood on the shrub- and tree-lined woodland path leading down to the lake, closely entwined and inadequately shielded from the gaze of potential witnesses who could not but disapprove because they would regard the sight that met their eyes as "sick and depraved"—the list of current descriptions was a long one. Jakob might not be acquainted with it yet, but Erneste was. Despite this, they not only kissed but began to touch whatever their hands could reach without interrupting their kiss, without severing the bond between their lips. Their hands roamed over shoulders and back, neck and hair, arms, hips and buttocks—or over the cloth, at least, that covered the flesh, sinews and muscles beneath.

It was Erneste who summoned up the courage to put his right hand on Jakob's penis, whose presence he had long felt. Without hesitation, unafraid of being repulsed, his hand enveloped the cloth beneath which Jakob's penis strained as powerfully, crudely and shockingly as his own.

Jakob didn't recoil. On the contrary, he pressed even closer, his penis sliding obediently through Erneste's fingers beneath the cloth. Erneste felt the glans, gripped the shaft, cupped his hand around Jakob's testicles. Jakob groaned aloud. Erneste stifled the sound with his lips. Jakob was trembling all over. No one had ever touched him where Erneste's hand now lay, and while the ball of Erneste's thumb moved slowly up and down between glans and shaft, navel and scrotum, his own hand soon found its way to Erneste's penis. He groaned again between two intakes of breath, and this time a sigh escaped his lips. To Erneste, his breath felt like a silken cloth fluttering in his ear.

It was little short of a miracle that no hotel guests or Sunday excursionists crossed their path during those five minutes of perfect bliss. If they had, there would undoubtedly have been a scandal. But Erneste and Jakob had the shameless good fortune to be alone in the world for a few moments, alone and unobserved. Nobody came their way, neither adult nor child. Had they been caught, they would have been dismissed the same day.

Erneste had recommended that Jakob, who felt condemned to inactivity at the sideboard, should be promoted to waiting table, and he'd eventually gotten his way. Monsieur Flamin, who hadn't failed to notice Jakob's courteous manner, was persuaded by Erneste to give him suitable employment, at first on the terrace and later in the dining room. He also, when required, provided room service.

Although Jakob's gratitude to Erneste was beyond doubt, it wasn't gratitude that had prompted him to kiss Erneste that afternoon. That kiss and embrace were an expression of some other emotion—how profound an emotion, time would tell. He must have known that his behavior represented a threat to himself as well as to Erneste, who found it an abiding mystery why he should so recklessly have exposed himself to the danger of discovery. Not wanting to shake Jakob's nerve, however, he refrained both then and later from inquiring why he had kissed him that first time, some halfway down to the lake, before they turned around and headed back to the hotel. They had detached themselves after a minute or two, but it was all they could do to keep their hands off each other.

It hadn't been hard to convince Monsieur Flamin, who had been observing him for long enough, of Jakob's talents. Having had a few words with him, Flamin announced that he was willing to give him an opportunity after only two months. A smart, good-looking young-ster—*un jeune homme adroit et flexible avec une pareille jolie gueule d'amour*—was always welcome. Had Monsieur Flamin seen the two of them at that moment, he might not have dismissed them even though there was no shortage of willing employees. He would merely have turned away and pretended not to see. Monsieur Flamin wasn't easily shocked.

———•◦•———

It was always the same images that haunted Erneste that night, whether awake or tossing to and fro in a state of semiwakefulness. They were and remained identical: two menacing reflections. He would have certainly been rid of them had he managed to turn on the light and get up, but he couldn't. He didn't turn on the light or get up, he lay prostrate, so the images persisted, flowing out of him and back again, drifting through him as he drifted through them. He didn't turn on the light, took no sleeping pill, waited, fell asleep, dreamed, woke up, dreamed again. It was interminable—an interminable, inescapable, exhausting cycle.

A light was on across the way, he knew. His shadowy neighbor, almost a shadow of himself, was pacing up and down. He knew this although he couldn't see her. While he was endeavoring to sleep she staunchly remained awake, and he saw two images in his dreams, one of today and one of the old days, both equally motionless, equally distinct, equally cold and crisp, one overlaying and suppressing the other. His soul felt the touch of ice and was touched by it, frozen and petrified.

One image was of Jakob standing motionless in front of the airliner, an image from his imagination, his imaginary image of that morning: a white airliner against a dark background. The other was of Jakob and himself. Not an imaginary image but the actual, authentic moment when they touched and kissed for the very first time. It was so close and clear in his mind's eye, the incident it represented might only just have occurred. He could feel the other tongue in his mouth without being aware of his own, could feel the pressure of the other body and only now became conscious of his own, a cold body, cold but not unfamiliar. The time of intimacy was long past, cold and incalculable, and the tongue in his mouth might have been composed of nothing—of wax. And while the first image might have signified how far apart they'd grown—he himself had never traveled by air—the other was an unmistakable indication that the gap between them hadn't widened by a millimeter since then. Even though the other body had become unfamiliar to him, it was unfamiliar but close at hand.

Such were the two images he couldn't shake off that night, which accompanied him into sleep and wrested him from it once more. He awoke and felt the pressure of his body, fell asleep and continued to feel it, but in either case, whether he was asleep or awake, the images were somber, not warm, not sunny like that summer afternoon in July 1935, but gloomy as the autumnal night that cheerlessly encompassed the town and its inhabitants, his neighbor, himself, and, somewhere or other, Jakob as well. There was darkness around them, darkness in front of the airplane, darkness behind it. Everything was as cold and dreary and confused as his life had been since Jakob's letter. His life had undergone a minuscule change: sleepy indifference had given way to hectic activity. He could no longer control his thoughts and emotions and hold them in check—couldn't control them at all. What he had left behind him lay ahead of him once more. It had simply been a comforting illusion to believe that he'd left his time with Jakob behind him; it had never been behind him. He had never left Jakob. Jakob was as present as if he had never gone away; Jakob and he were mutually pervasive. That, at any rate, was what Erneste felt between waking and dreaming in the small hours, after he had opened and read Jakob's second letter.

It was somewhat longer than the first and made a confused impression. Jakob seemed to have written in great haste. Erneste didn't know what to make of it. He knew nothing of America and took no interest in politics, which had so far failed to bring him any luck.

Jakob's second letter read:

My dear Erneste,

I'm writing you again, quicker this time. You haven't had long to wait. But as you know, I'm still awaiting a reply from you. Perhaps our letters will cross, which is what I'd expect of a true friend. On the other hand, perhaps you haven't replied because you don't believe me or want anything more to do with me. I don't know much about you, but I do know you aren't married. You can't hide from me. Does our past mean nothing to you? Why else haven't you written? Have you seen Klinger? Haven't you written because you've already had a word with him? If so, I'd like to know what he told you. It may well be lies. Lying is his profession, after all. If not, what are you waiting for? I don't have any time to lose, unlike you. Tell him they're after me because of him. If the FBI (the police, in other words) are after me, it's because of him. They're the same people who were after him before—they thought he was a communist sympathizer. Now they're after me, the same men who were after Klinger: Weston, Broadhurst, Burlington, and the rest of those scum. He knows them too, they're still alive. Mention their names to him and you'll see. They've all come crawling back out of the woodwork. He had dealings with them. They'll arrest me if I don't get away in time. Either that or I'll have to bribe them. I need money if I'm to get away from here. I don't suppose you have any money, but Klinger has. He's well-heeled, he can help me.

Go and have a word with him. In my lousy life, every minute counts. I'm sure you won't let your Jakob down.

Love,

Jack/Jakob Meier.

Monsieur Flamin was extremely satisfied with Jakob's work, as was only to be expected. Jakob did more than his duties prescribed. He was attentive, skillful and quick. He did the donkey-work for other members of staff and was capable of making decisions himself if need be. Monsieur Flamin and Herr Direktor Wagner admired his initiative, his respect for authority, his quick-wittedness, and, last but not least, his unwavering composure. He seemed to have no personal quality that did *not* merit admiration, and even his less admirable qualities might have been tolerated—and certainly would have been by Erneste—had they come to light. Erneste's admiration for his beloved friend did not diminish; on the contrary, it grew with every passing day. There was nothing he wouldn't have forgiven the love of his life, but there was nothing to forgive, not yet. Erneste could detect no flaws in Jakob, only virtues.

Jakob had long ceased to be dependent on Erneste's advice when he was finally, at the beginning of September, permitted to wait table in the dining room as well. The nights had become distinctly cooler, so dinner was no longer served on the terrace. The guests now dined indoors, where they could continue to dress lightly for a while. There was still a touch of summer in the air, even after nightfall, when the menfolk went out onto the terrace after dinner, or more rarely between courses, to chat and smoke in peace.

Jakob left the terrace, which had become his kingdom, and conquered a new one. He and Erneste were universally popular, especially with female guests and more particularly with unaccompanied widows. It was pleasantest of all to be served by both of them at once. What elegant, handsome young men they were—so much better-looking than all the men of their acquaintance—and what good manners and nice skin they had! If the ladies hadn't aspired to more ambitious careers for their own children, and if they hadn't realized that not even waiters stay young forever, they might almost have felt inclined to want them as sons-in-law.

Before long, Jakob was past teaching anything anymore. He had mastered all the tricks of the trade. His smattering of French was cute, his English charming, his deportment impeccable. He had quickly become a perfect waiter, one who could unhesitatingly have been employed in the finest establishments, so the tips he received were lavish. Their munificence was far from inappropriate, given that money cannot be more profitably invested than in one's personal comfort, and not only on vacation.

Jakob was not only a perfect waiter but a perfect lover. Erneste's chagrin at not being the only person to enjoy his favors was still to come. In September of 1935 he had Jakob's affection all to himself.

There were two times of day for Erneste: working hours and the few hours he and Jakob spent unobserved in their little room, a domain to which no one but they had access. It was dark in there, but light enough for them. Chambermaids had no business entering their room, which had running water, so they kept it clean themselves. They were issued fresh towels and bed linen once a month.

During working hours Erneste thought of that other time, the time after work, of nighttime and his other, separate life. And when he passed Jakob at work he thought he discerned in his eyes the same expectancy that made his own heart beat faster, the same yearning for the night to come, the same longing for a second, brief—far too brief—time of day, for the physical contact possible only in the seclusion of their little room, where both of them shared the same desire. Anyone watching them closely must have noticed that the looks they exchanged were more than just friendly. They couldn't make physical contact during work, but whenever they chanced to pass one another in a doorway or stand side by side in front of the cutlery drawer, they contrived to brush hands or elbows, even hips or thighs. This, too, was seen only by those who chose to see it, in other words, by those who habitually detect something equivocal—or thoroughly unequivocal, depending on their point of view—in everything and everyone. The other waiters treated them with friendly indifference. The others were content with their own, limited horizon, and off duty that seldom encompassed their immediate surroundings, which were unimportant compared to what awaited them back home: girlfriends or wives and families in places no one else had ever seen.

The one time—their hours of work—seemed neverending, whereas the other time—nighttime—passed in a flash. The nights, which seldom began before midnight, were a princely recompense for all those working hours, but they were short. Erneste still found it hard to believe in his ownership of that other body. As he surrendered his body to Jakob, so Jakob's was his to possess. Neither of them made any attempt to play coy or hold back. They would eventually fall asleep after all their talk and exertions, Erneste slumped against Jakob's shoulder and Jakob with his head on one side.

If the days were too long, the nights were too short. The nights seemed to run away with them, escaping their love and leaving behind a dull ache which sometimes became so intense that Erneste started to weep. The two of them had to get up at six, often after no more than three hours' sleep, because there were always a few guests who wanted their breakfast served at seven.

At night they found it easy to forget their work and their subordinate status. Then, for the first time, they were free: two runaway slaves in an expanse of green meadow very like the Alpine pasture conjured up by the painter of a picture hanging in the breakfast room, a meadow backed by snow-capped peaks.

They rose at six and washed in a hurry, suppressed their mounting desire or failed to suppress it, washed again, put on their waiters' outfits, knotted their bow ties, and combed each other's hair because that was quicker than doing it in the mirror. Each was at pains to see that the other looked spruce. Before parting they kissed, with the result that their lips were temporarily redder than those of their colleagues, who would already be waiting for them with impassive faces. They often turned up a few minutes late, their hair still slick with the saliva they'd used to tame each other's rebellious locks. They were happy beyond a doubt. Fate was favoring them. The situation couldn't last forever, but it lasted a little while longer.

———

Sometimes, when Jakob passed Erneste in the lobby or dining room or out on the terrace, or when he lay down beside him at night, Erneste had to fight back the tears. Sometimes he failed to do so, but Jakob couldn't see this in the darkness. There was no electric light in their room. If they needed light they lit a candle. The moon shone on the front of the building, not into their cramped little attic at the rear, which just had room for two beds, a wardrobe and two chairs. The chairs were used merely as clothes-horses, hardly ever for sitting on.

Erneste may already have sensed that his happiness wouldn't last forever, but that wasn't the only reason for his tears. He wept simply because he was happy, and he was happy because he loved Jakob—because of Jakob's nearness and the touch of Jakob's hand on his lips, his chest, his belly, his thighs. He slept and awoke in a state of bliss; no other word would do. They were tired, the work was strenuous and the days were long. They seemed particularly long at the height of the season in 1935. July of that year was an exceptionally busy time. Numerous guests—refugees—had arrived from Germany. Quiet, inoffensive, apprehensive people who sometimes got drunk, they lingered in Giessbach, unable to decide when to leave and where to go.

When the moment finally came—when Erneste was lying beside Jakob in bed after midnight—he would fall asleep exhausted in his arms, and Jakob would be asleep already.

It was a long time since Erneste had wept. He occasionally shed silent tears at the movies, but they were just a reflex response to an unreal sorrow of absolutely no significance, neither oppressive nor cathartic. His eyes were dry by the time the lights went up. He had also wept back then, when his tears stemmed less from fear of the future than from the happiness he currently felt. But that was long ago. Those thirty years had passed like a day.

6

Why hadn't he thought of it before? When it finally occurred to him, the burden that had weighed him down for days and weeks on end fell from his shoulders like a grain of sand, making room for other thoughts—lucid, liberating thoughts. One idea, one new and really quite simple idea, had been enough to present everything in a new light. So that was the answer, a sudden flash of inspiration, but one that must be put into effect without delay. It was as if he'd finally come of age.

With that, Jakob receded until the distance between them became bearable. His image didn't entirely disappear, but it lost definition and no longer stood in his way. Erneste was alone now. He had only to do what had to be done in the correct order, and everything else would follow. He had only to sit down at the kitchen table, put a sheet of paper in front of him, take a ballpoint, and write that he had now decided not to call Klinger, not to look him up or cadge money from him. He, Erneste, was leading his own life, and there was no room in that life for Jakob or Klinger—neither for you, Jakob, nor for the man who touched, seduced and stole you from me. You went away with him, so go after him, go after him yourself, preserve your devotion to him, don't depend on me, be his servant, don't rely on my help, be his property. You left me forever; now I'm leaving you forever. The thing I couldn't until today believe would happen has happened: you're out of my life at last for good and all, and it's a relief.

The sentences he meant to write took shape in his mind, but they took shape so fast, and there was so many of them, that he was soon incapable of registering them all. They grew longer, and the longer they grew the less he understood them himself, and what was unintelligible to him would certainly be unintelligible to Jakob. And then it was as if they were trying to erase one another. The faster they occurred to him, the more this process of mutual erasure continued. One sentence gobbled up the next, yet they multiplied instead of becoming fewer. In lieu of a few well-organized sentences, whole concatenations of sentences took shape, and he knew he would never manage to memorize the best and most hurtful of them. That was why he had to write them down as soon as possible, but for that he needed some paper and a pen. As soon as he had a ballpoint in his hand at home, the right words—the ones that had slipped his memory—would come back to him. But he wasn't at home, not yet, because first he had something else in mind: a form of diversion and release—one of those escapades in which he had indulged for many years and at fairly regular intervals. Midnight came as the words continued to wing their way through his head and out again, like arrows, and just as midnight came he made his way past the statue beside the entrance to the park, the one he'd passed so many times before, a bare-breasted mother weeping over her dying child, and heard the familiar sounds he'd so often heard before: stealthy footsteps, a stifled groan, the rasp of a match as it flared up and went out, momentarily illuminating the features of some unknown man. A few whispered words were exchanged, a door opened to reveal white tiles and shadowy figures moving around in front of them. Then it softly closed again. The door of the toilet, used only by his own kind from early evening onward, was a universal center of interest. Insofar as they were still looking because they hadn't yet found anything, all eyes were focused on that door. The light threw figures into relief, but not faces. When the door opened, a strip of light slanted across the gravel path. The door closed and swallowed the light, opened and spit it out again a hundred times a night.

The air was filled with subdued sounds. The toilet's telltale light, which never went out, illuminated the park's activities for the benefit even of those who took no part in them—for those who watched those peculiar goings-on with the arrogance of wholesome distaste, or with the official curiosity displayed by the police when they raided the toilet at irregular intervals. They invariably arrested a few frightened, middle-aged men—married men with children, more often than not—and released them a few hours later.

He'd been inspired to write to Jakob by a casual remark

from Julie the last time they'd met before she returned to Paris. "I really enjoy writing to Steve," she'd told him over dinner at the restaurant. "Why don't I write to you more often? I wouldn't have to write to you in secret, after all. For that matter, why don't you ever write to me?" His cousin had fiddled continuously with her rings and bracelets as she spoke.

He should now have been concentrating on what mattered, but he couldn't. Not because the hour was so late, or because he'd split a bottle of wine with Julie, or because he was distracted by what was going on around him, but simply because he couldn't grasp the essentials. As soon as he thought he'd captured them they escaped. The essentials didn't exist, or only if they were surrounded by irrelevancies that would throw them into sharp relief like the men silhouetted against the light in the public toilet. Perhaps everything was irrelevant save death. The death of love signified the advent of death, the advent of love the demise of death.

He really wanted his letter to Jakob to convey the crux of the matter in a few words, a few irrefutable words that would negate any attempt at self-justification—indeed, defy all contradiction. As it was, the words proliferated until the letter he'd been beating his brains about since saying goodbye to Julie became more and more muddled. So far, the innumerable sentences they formed existed only in his head. Jakob, who was meant to read, understand, and be moved and reduced to silence by them, wouldn't understand a thing unless he could rein them back on paper. And what a defeat that would be, given that the whole point was to bring home to Jakob, at long last, what he'd done to him. But he didn't want, either, to disguise the fact that he might have suffered all too willingly, and that he was partly responsible for the duration of his suffering because of the persistence with which he'd clung to it. He would write that too. He didn't want to complain, but he didn't want to deny the truth either. Jakob must be compelled to realize what a mistake he'd made by leaving him and going away with Klinger. He'd thought he'd hit the jackpot, but he'd drawn a blank in the end, just like Erneste. America had brought him no luck.

A few words would have to suffice. Erneste wanted their brevity to be a lethal weapon that would reduce Jakob to silence forever, not only the strange new Jakob in America, but the one inside his head. He wanted to liberate himself from that one most of all. Jakob must realize how serious he was and how little he knew of the torment he'd suppressed for decades—decades! But he would mention that torment only in passing. The more casual their tone, the more effective his words would be.

Just then Erneste was grabbed from behind and jerked backward. He lost his balance, conscious of the viselike pressure of an arm clamped around his throat. The steely embrace cut off his breath and circulation. A thick, colorless curtain came down and he passed out, but not before hearing a voice whisper two words in his ear: "Cocksucker, buttfucker."

He was lying on the floor when he recovered consciousness. Unsurprised, he fought for breath as he lay there on his back. He could hear himself gasping, hear his own hoarse breathing. Then he was hit with some heavy object, some kind of cudgel, first in the chest, then in the stomach. He curled up on his side, but no sooner had he done so than someone kicked him in the ribs. So there was more than one of them. He heard shouts nearby, but not for long. They were scared of attracting the attention of outsiders and alerting the police. Erneste wasn't the only one they'd picked on for their night's entertainment. Two or three others had also failed to make a run for it in time. There were several assailants, three at least. They never came alone and were always armed with weapons of some kind.

What he had always dreaded had now come to pass: they had caught him. Now he was in it up to his neck. They would kick and beat him senseless.

Too engrossed in his own thoughts, which were unconnected with his personal safety, he hadn't been alert or quick enough. He hadn't heard them coming or detected their lurking presence. They wanted their fun and they were having it. They beat up on anyone in the park they could catch, and they would go on doing so for as long as they thought fit. They alone would determine the duration of this orgy of violence. They were young and strong and convinced of the unimpeachable nature of what they were doing.

They usually turned up on weekends, but today was

Thursday. Warm, viscous blood was oozing from his nose and mouth. How on earth could he appear for work with a swollen nose and split lips?

Another blow, a faint, crunching sound from beneath the skin, and he passed out again. That was his temporary salvation.

The next time he recovered consciousness he at once took in the fact that four men were standing over him. They were concentrating on him alone. "Pervert!" they growled. "Filthy queer!" Erneste felt as if he was lying with his head in a dog turd, but what did that matter in his predicament? Why worry about that, of all things?

There was a lot of raucous laughter. He didn't catch what else was said because a thick, soundproof wall had muffled every sound. Kicks were being delivered. Each of the men was at liberty to kick him as often and in as many places as he chose. It's always the same, he thought: first you have a good idea, then a bad one. Strangely enough, only his assailants seemed to be really with it; he himself could scarcely feel a thing.

Perhaps one of the many blows he'd sustained had rendered him insensitive to all the blows that followed. Perhaps that crucial blow had struck, severed and deactivated a special nerve essential to the experiencing of pain. His body felt alien to him. Although he was lying helpless on the floor, he took a long stride, and after that he found himself in another world, and every succeeding blow reinforced his position in that other world. Another blow, and another, or no blow at all—it didn't matter, he felt none of them. One connected with his knee, another with his genitals, another with his head again. They had stamina, his assailants, you had to grant them that much. He couldn't see their faces. They continued to aim deliberate, almost desperate blows at him, a squirming figure that might or might not have been screaming as well—he couldn't hear—but seemed curiously absent. He was elsewhere, but he probably wouldn't die; the frontier he'd just crossed gave access to deserted terrain, a rendezvous for the insensitive. He was in a state of drunken dissolution, not a permanent condition but one that fortunately persisted. Then it went dark again. Jakob and the letter, Klinger and America, Julie and his own uninteresting existence—all had disappeared. Everything within him concentrated on remaining in that other world.

The noise had almost died down by the time he came to again. Guffawing, they unzipped their flies. What better way of demonstrating their superiority, what more effective display of contempt, than to wisecrack as they pissed on him? They must have been drinking beer, because it was two or three minutes before they strode out, one of them whistling a popular tune. They'd had an enjoyable Thursday night. Everything had gone the way they'd hoped, maybe even better.

A church clock struck once just as he tried to get to his feet. It had to be one o'clock or half-past. He was overcome by the pain he'd been spared until now.

His attempt to get up seemed to rend him in two. He

collapsed. He couldn't stand, couldn't walk, couldn't call for help. No sound escaped his lips, just a trickle of blood. He was doomed to pick up the thread they'd extracted from his body: he wasn't dead.

No morning newspaper would report what had happened here. He was alone, the others had gone, no one could help him, no one would tend him. He should go to the hospital, but he wouldn't. The urine was beginning to evaporate and leave a sticky film on his skin. Unable to suppress his nausea, he vomited, soiling his jacket and trousers. It was self-loathing that eventually lent him the strength to stand up. He had to. His clothes were sodden, torn and filthy like his inner self—there was no difference. His one thought was to get away from there, to get up, go home and wash, sluice off the filth they'd soiled him with. He was soiled. That wouldn't wash off so quickly, but he must make a start. He must wash, shower, soak in the bathtub, lie there until the stench of blood and urine and vomit had disappeared from this cramped world of his, until the scent of soap had displaced the stench of humiliation.

Back on his feet at last, he essayed a first few faltering steps. It might take him hours to reach home.

When he awoke the next morning he made up his mind to pay Klinger a visit. He wouldn't write to Jakob for the time being.

7

They said goodbye on the platform in Basel on October 15, 1935. Erneste's memory of that occasion was as vivid as his memory of their first meeting on the landing stage beside the Lake of Brienz. They shook hands and went their separate ways amid countless people hurrying from somewhere to somewhere else, and although they knew and had assured each other that they weren't saying goodbye forever, this parting would later prove to have set an almost casual seal on their mutual love, which wouldn't revive as Erneste hoped when they saw each other again, or only on his side. Their heyday was over.

Erneste was disheartened by what happened six months later, when they met by arrangement and shook hands again on the very same platform in Basel station, for Jakob's manner, when they confronted each other again after all those months, was cold and aloof. Erneste tried to persuade himself that it was only natural to feel a certain initial strangeness after a long separation, but he couldn't fail to notice that Jakob almost imperceptibly shrank away from him.

Although he clung for a while to the belief that their relationship would continue, that it could be revived or resurrected in some way, Jakob had quite simply changed. He was six months older, six months more mature. He had seen his family again and mingled with people whom he never mentioned, but who had exerted an influence on him. Nothing else could account for his transformation, within six months, into a reticent young man.

But that lay in the future. It was still October, and there was no doubt that Jakob, too, believed that their happiness would endure and their reunion be unconstrained. A handshake under the gaze of strangers before whom they observed the social conventions—that handshake was all they permitted themselves when saying goodbye in the fall of 1935. They refrained from any more intimate physical contact, for instance an embrace of the kind permissible between brothers. They might have been mistaken for brothers had they kissed each other on the cheek, but they didn't, afraid that even the most innocent gesture might give them away.

The season in Giessbach was over. The hotel got no sun during the winter, so it remained closed until the spring. The place was too bleak and inhospitable for guests at this time of year, but Herr Direktor Wagner and his wife, together with his secretary and the cellarman, a local from Brienz, remained on the premises to catch up on the paperwork that had been neglected during the summer months, ensure that the pipes didn't freeze up, and guard against pilfering. Where the rest of the staff were concerned, the majority would not be back before the middle of March. Although there were countless hotels in Thun, Interlaken and Lucerne where they could probably have found work, most of them scattered to the four winds. The *saisonniers*, or seasonal workers, either went home to their families, where they spent the winter as prosperous citizens envied by their impoverished friends and relations, or sought work at luxury hotels far afield, where they usually performed menial and ill-paid jobs for which they were rewarded with good references. Glad of a brief escape from the uneventfulness of life in the country, they undoubtedly led an easier, freer existence in the towns. But when their thoughts harked back to Giessbach, as they often did after only a few days, they felt faintly nostalgic for the lake, the forest and the cascades, with the result that they were happy to return in spring to the place they had blithely left in the fall. All except for Erneste, who was anything but happy to have to leave Giessbach and the room he'd been sharing with Jakob.

Erneste went to Paris, as he had in previous years. He'd failed to convince Jakob how essential it was to continue their joint existence in an attic room at the Lutétia, the Meurisse, or some other Parisian hotel where he could easily have found his friend a job had he wanted one. But Jakob was homesick for Germany. He listened attentively but remained adamant, determined to go home and show off his new-found skills. Now that full employment prevailed in Germany, he said, he would be bound to find a well-paid job at the Domhotel or some other establishment in Cologne. And so it turned out: he spent five months working in a senior position at the Savoy.

So Jakob went back to Germany, where his family and friends were impatient to see him again, or so he claimed. Although the only mail he'd received during his months at Giessbach were two postcards from his mother, which he showed Erneste without comment, he steadfastly insisted how essential it was for him to return to Cologne and be reunited with his mother, his family and friends—friends whom he'd never mentioned and who had never written to him. He'd heard and read so much about the improved conditions in Germany under the new regime, he wanted to see them for himself. Jakob had expressed this sudden interest in the changes back home after picking up one or two details from hotel guests and the newspapers. He had spoken of Hitler and Goebbels and the forthcoming Berlin Olympics, and Erneste had no reason to doubt that his interest was genuine.

Yet it had seemed to him that Jakob was speaking from behind a mask, telling lies in ignorance of what to conceal. This feeling might merely have been an expression of Erneste's deep but possibly quite unjustified concern, a symptom of the pain of separation. On the other hand, perhaps his impression really was well-founded.

So Jakob had struck him, even then, as remote, and this alarmed him. He seemed remote because he was trying to detach himself. Wasn't that it? Wasn't that what worried him?

Erneste, who hadn't mourned his parents' death and had little appreciation of Jakob's homesickness, let him go instead of trying to restrain him. He left him standing on the platform. Had he clung to him, Jakob might well have shaken him off, and that would have hurt more than any other form of separation. Unable to restrain Jakob, he'd had to let him go.

"Till next year. See you at the end of March—late March or early April." Those had been Jakob's parting words on the platform, so Erneste had had no need to say them himself. It was clear from Jakob's tone that he really meant them, and that he hoped to pick up the thread where they had been compelled to leave it. Yes, he was being sincere, and perhaps everything would turn out the way they'd so often envisioned in the foregoing days and nights: nothing would have changed when they saw each other again; their temporary separation would be only a minor obstacle on their way into the future, and no more to be avoided than the future itself.

———•—•———

Erneste had known he couldn't count on getting any mail from Jakob, or a New Year's card at most. One week after New Year's, if not before, he realized he couldn't expect even that. It wasn't the fault of the mails. The fault lay with Jakob himself, with the distractions that were claiming his time, with his friends and family, perhaps with his work. Perhaps it also had something to do with the turn of the year, which was celebrated quite differently in Germany than in France.

Although Erneste had already written Jakob several postcards and some letters—which he fervently hoped his mother hadn't opened—Jakob had never replied. He had no choice but to endure Jakob's silence patiently. But his patience ran out after only an hour or two. For the rest of the day, not only while at work but even more intensely when off duty, he thought of nothing but Jakob. In the end he couldn't dismiss the notion that Jakob was being unfaithful to him just as he himself had briefly been tempted, for a few days only, to fall for a youngster employed at the Lutétia as an elevator attendant. Their relationship had remained purely physical, however, because his hankering for Jakob soon became too much for him and he broke it off after their fourth assignation.

Those winter months in Paris had left no lasting impressions behind. Discounting the elevator attendant, his memory of them was almost a blank. If he preserved any general recollection of them, it resembled an aftertaste rather than a palpable image. There was no room in it for the place where he had hoped to spend the winter with Jakob. In Paris he had already been leading the lonely existence in which he would later make his permanent home. Together with his little affair, it foreshadowed what was to come, but of that he was still unaware.

He had sometimes been afraid, when even more depressed than usual, that he would never see Jakob again, so he was relieved as much as overjoyed when, on April 26, 1936, they were reunited in the same station and on the same platform where they had exchanged a farewell handshake six months before, the difference being that even more people were hurrying to and fro, this time without coats or scarfs because it was a really warm spring day. And this time he found it even harder not to take Jakob in his arms. It was all he could do not to kiss him on the neck, possibly the body's most sensitive area.

At that moment, although the hour hand of the station clock had rotated over four thousand times in the previous six months, Erneste fancied that it had registered the same lapse of time in a single, whirlwind circuit of the dial. He was standing just where he had stood six months earlier, never having budged from the spot. The passers-by had changed their clothes, but that was all. Whatever had happened in the interim didn't matter—it meant nothing: the hands hadn't moved an inch, nor had he, nor had Jakob. But the belief that nothing had changed was a fleeting illusion. It was soon borne in on Erneste that almost everything had changed.

His winter in Paris, with its lingering disappointment, tedious work and short-lived affair, was obliterated when he gripped Jakob's hand and released it. The warmth of their handshake seemed to convey that they had never been apart. But then, as he looked into Jakob's eyes, he was overcome with despair. It was Jakob's green eyes that inspired this feeling. They seemed to have seen things of which he would never speak.

At the same time, he had become even more handsome, a young man with the firm handshake of an adult who smiled at Erneste in a slightly detached and condescending manner. Although Erneste knew nothing, and his ignorance threatened to choke him, the one thing he grasped at that moment was that this new and unfamiliar Jakob was going to leave him, possibly even for a woman. Not today or tomorrow, perhaps, but sooner or later. He felt puny and insignificant—a nobody compared to this tall, good-looking young man whom he would never succeed in capturing and keeping. No matter how much security and affection he offered, Jakob would always remain one step ahead of him.

Had he turned on his heel, his life would have taken a different direction. Not that he knew it, he was merely prolonging the agony.

8

He sometimes caught himself yearning for the authentic Jakob while the real one was lying beside him. Although he could feel the warmth of him, he kept thinking of the Jakob who had left him behind on the platform in Basel and then, far away in Cologne, dissolved into thin air. Jakob's body, which he knew even better than his own, seemed to have been inhabited by a stranger since his return from Germany. His voice was still the same, but his way of speaking and the words he used to convey what he saw and heard were different.

He had developed a cocky manner unseemly in a waiter, no matter how handsome and popular. Erneste, who was concerned for Jakob's career and reputation, was distressed by this and tried to make this clear to him. "Be careful what you say, Jakob," he told him a couple of times, and: "Jakob, don't talk so big, people don't like it." But it was no use, Jakob just smiled and rubbed his right eye with his forefinger or rested his hand on Erneste's belly and said, "If you say so." He was too self-assured to be impressed by Erneste's warning that he would sooner or later get into serious trouble with Herr Direktor

Wagner or with one of the guests. But he didn't get into trouble, even though he wasn't his former self. The changes Erneste perceived in him failed to impair his popularity; on the contrary, they seemed to enhance it.

Erneste was compelled to accept that this Jakob was the only one who now inhabited the body that never refused itself to him, day or night. Yet he clung to the hope that the real Jakob would one day reoccupy this body he knew so well, as if he had simply been away for a while. He could hold that body, but nothing more. What lay hidden within it escaped his grasp. It was a stranger who lay beside him, and he pined for the Jakob he knew and had lost, who was hidden behind the stranger's façade. The new Jakob was merely granting him a reprieve. He loved the old Jakob, but the old one had gone.

Erneste felt sure that Jakob would leave him sooner or later. He knew his fate and wouldn't fight it. Fate was taking its course despite him.

The changes in Jakob had their advantages as well. The pleasure he gave Erneste became ever more intense, night after night. This, Erneste assumed, had to do with his winter in Cologne, where he had learned things of which they never spoke. He had developed an almost insatiable appetite, and since there was nobody else around to assuage it, Erneste was the one who ensured that he eventually drifted off to sleep. But for Jakob's daily demands to satisfy him regardless of all else, Erneste might have gone mad—mad for love of the real Jakob, whom he had lost and couldn't rediscover. But this may have been an idea that didn't occur to him until later on, when it was all over and he had been forced to acknowledge that the letter he craved from America would never come. Meantime, what mattered in Giessbach was to satisfy the requirements of the guests who were now arriving in unprecedented numbers. The demand for rooms was so great that applicants had to be turned away daily, especially as regular guests were given precedence. It was as if the whole world wanted to assemble at Giessbach's Grand Hotel before disintegrating into its separate components.

Most of the guests came from Germany, many of them being Jews who had managed to get all or at least some of their assets out of the country and were now waiting at the Grand, either for a British or American visa, or for speedy permission to settle in Switzerland, or for a fundamental change in the political situation in Germany. The latter was a vain hope, and there was little prospect of acquiring a Swiss resident's permit, which was not particularly sought-after in any case, given that one couldn't feel much safer in Switzerland than elsewhere in Europe. The Germans, as Jakob, too, reported, were going after all their potential enemies, particularly the Jews, who had been subject to special legislation since the previous September. But there were also guests who would naturally return to Germany in due course because there was no reason for them to leave the country for good. This resulted in the formation of cliques that either mingled or shunned each other's company, and Monsieur Flamin had to employ all his strategic skill in seating guests appropriately, not only in the dining room but more particularly in the far smaller breakfast room, because some of them were afraid of eavesdroppers, even though many of the people they felt in need of protection from were harmless elderly couples. Appearances could be deceptive—they were Germans, after all—but the real danger, everyone agreed, came from the younger ones. Monsieur Flamin knew what had to be done and he did it with a touch of pleasure at his ability to resolve awkward situations.

So Erneste and Jakob and all their many fellow employees were kept at full stretch, with little time to reflect on their personal circumstances. A strange euphoria seemed to prevail, mainly among the younger guests—a mixture of frivolity and fear, dejection and optimism. They were happy to have escaped, even if they didn't know where they would end up, because all were now convinced that another war was inevitable. Some of them, who had only become acquainted in Giessbach, often sat talking in the bar until all hours. Jakob told Erneste where they came from and what they talked about. He had been the first to volunteer for night duty behind the bar because he wanted to see "the international set", as he put it.

———·•·———

Julius Klinger turned up in June of 1936, accompanied by his wife and two children. His arrival caused more of a stir than that of any other guest from Germany, and not only because he was famous. Apart from Erneste and the other foreign employees, everyone in Giessbach seemed to know his name, even Jakob, who had never read a word Klinger had written. Jakob said that every child in Germany knew of him. His novels had been filmed, he said, and he went on to quote the titles of various books and movies that meant nothing to Erneste, who had long ago forgotten the titles of any movies he'd seen, and in most cases their story lines as well.

On June 19, 1936, after rumors of Klinger's arrival had been circulating for several days, some thirty people gathered in the hotel lobby to applaud him and, by their very presence, express gratitude for his unenforced and principled stand against the Nazis. Although Klinger had until recently, and even during the war of 1914–18, refrained from any political utterances, he had now come out openly against Germany's new rulers, whom he abominated. To the refugees who stood in the lobby and applauded his arrival, he represented the true values of the country they'd reluctantly been compelled to leave. He had refused to be swayed, either by flattery on the part of the regime, or by attempts to exert pressure on him.

Julius Klinger's books had not been publicly burned in Germany, just ignored. Three weeks before leaving for Giessbach, he had decided to break his silence with all the force inherent in a single sentence. His letter addressed to Goebbels on May 20, 1936, had appeared in Switzerland's *Neue Zürcher Zeitung*. It contained no word of reproach or accusation, yet it caused more of a stir, both at home and abroad, than he had expected—and this despite its brevity, which rendered it all the more effective. Perfectly suited to being quoted in the foreign press, his letter was published even in the *New York Times*.

Quite a few people who had already left the country were beginning to have doubts about Klinger's much-invoked integrity, but when they learned of his letter, and certainly when they learned of its contents, the tide promptly turned in his favor. Interest centered not only on him, but also on those who had been expelled from Germany. He had chosen the right moment to do what was expected of him. With a single sentence—"We true Germans will have to show you the error of your ways; we have no choice"—he had invoked the decent Germany they personified and attested the rightness of their actions. He had even, in a way, affirmed that Jews who no longer possessed any rights inside Germany were the people best qualified to uphold true German values beyond its borders until the advent of better times, when they would be summoned home again.

Klinger's letter contained no threat; it was universally construed as a warning. Whether he was alluding between the lines to his own potential departure from Germany, to which he actually made no reference, remained a moot point and was also the subject of heated arguments at Giessbach. For want of any better idea, Goebbels lambasted him like a dog barking after an intruder has fled: Klinger was what he had always believed him to be, a decadent, Jewified snob whose literary heyday had ended long ago. "You're a man of the last century: we don't need your kind. Go and try your luck with the Bolsheviks!"

Erneste heard all these things from Jakob, who never tired of telling him what was discussed at night in the hotel bar—where Klinger never showed his face, incidentally. He and his wife, who never drank except at meals, retired to bed early, immediately after dinner as a rule. Unlike them, their children mingled with the other guests as a matter of course. The Klingers evidently had no objection to this, although the boy was seventeen at most but looked older. The daughter was reputed to be an artist, not that anyone ever saw her with a sketchbook. She seemed to be as much at a loose end as her brother. The boy was still of school age, but present circumstances entailed that he would be tutored by his mother and sister until further notice. He was said to have artistic leanings, so Jakob told Erneste, and no wonder, with parents like his, but although there were pianos in the ballroom and breakfast room he had never been seen to play them. That his mother no longer performed in public was well known. Before the birth of her daughter in 1916 she had sung at Berlin's Lindenoper under Richard Strauss and then, after four seasons, unexpectedly retired. However, two recordings of her existed: *Ah, ma petite table!* on one side and *Voi che sapete* on the other. Julius Klinger, who much preferred the German repertoire, had for some time been in close touch with Richard Wagner's widow Cosima. This was because, before the outbreak of the Great War and the success of his second novel, *Oporta*, he had toyed with the idea—which never came to fruition—of writing a biography of his favorite composer in the style of a novel.

Klinger had not been arrested in Berlin despite his letter to Goebbels. He was allowed to leave the country for fear of reactions abroad, and also, no doubt, because the Nazis were relieved to be rid of him. No one could have foreseen what he would later assert in his only autobiographical essay, which devoted a few sentences to the subject. This was that during the first two weeks of his stay at the Grand Hotel in Giessbach, which he specifically mentioned in this context, he had been counting on a coup d'état. He had set off for Switzerland firmly convinced that certain senior German generals would shortly bring the madness in their country to an end, and he had no reason to mistrust those who had informed him that a putsch was imminent. In the event, however, Klinger waited for it as vainly as the rest of the world. No upheaval occurred, Hitler remained in power, the Germans were content, and Klinger spent several more weeks in Giessbach, during which time he made preparations to emigrate and worked on his latest book. He couldn't remain idle, being admired not least for the sheer magnitude of his output. He wrote and corrected several pages of manuscript a day. His work, his writing, was as essential to him as the air he breathed.

People became accustomed to his presence as time went by. His appearance at meals ceased to attract much attention—less attention, certainly, than that of his offspring, whose extravagant wardrobes seemed absolutely inexhaustible, whereas Klinger himself was notable only for his well-cut suits and English shoes and his wife mainly for her dark curls and dark-brown eyes. Marianne Klinger was "of Mediterranean appearance", as her husband put it, but she could also have been mistaken for a Jewess. A short woman, she had become somewhat plump after the birth of her son Maximilian, but her legs still drew appreciative male stares. The only guests to maintain a certain interest in Klinger were new arrivals, who were always trying to exchange a few words with him. This wasn't easy, and not only because he tended to address strangers in a very low voice. In contrast to his children, he avoided chance encounters as far as possible. When they became unavoidable he would shake hands and sign books, smiling amiably, but he refused to inscribe his name on menus or sheets of notepaper.

Two weeks after their arrival the Klingers were joined by Frau Moser, their Berlin housekeeper, who would later accompany them into exile. Erneste met her at the landing stage with two junior waiters. In addition to a wardrobe trunk, five suitcases had to be conveyed to the hotel. A quiet young woman who never wore make-up, Frau Moser moved into a small room in the hotel and took her meals at the Klingers' table. Certain guests viewed this with disapproval and incomprehension. Since she looked less like an employee than an underprivileged member of the family, however, even the most loudly disapproving guests eventually became inured to her presence in the dining room, especially as she never ventured to speak unless expressly asked a question by Klinger or his wife. The rest of the time she remained silent. She made a demure, reserved impression, quite unlike the young Klingers, who were always the first to get up and go, sometimes even while their parents were still at the dessert stage. According to Erneste, who was responsible for the family's table, Klinger seemed quite unaware of their bad manners, whereas his wife noticed but did nothing about them. It didn't disturb her, either, if Klinger started to smoke while she was still eating, nor did she persist when she failed to get an answer to her questions. Yet she never looked resentful or offended. She struck Erneste as a kindly and considerate but rather inscrutable woman. Despite the couple's middle-class exterior, some thought they detected a lingering trace of bohemianism in them because they had once belonged to that unconventional world, he as a novelist and she as a singer. And although they had divested themselves of all outward signs of their colorful past when they married, if not before, they remained artists still—and to the other guests that naturally excused many of their little quirks, which were really only trivial.

Erneste did not find waiting on the Klingers particularly congenial, so he offered no objection when Jakob, who waited table at the other end of the room, asked to take over from him. He sympathized with Jakob's interest in the German author, although Klinger never seemed to notice hotel staff even when they gave him a light or pushed his chair in. Besides, Erneste had meantime made a discovery that rendered it easy for him to move to the other end of the dining room.

Julius Klinger was a perceptive but hypersensitive person, a man who saw it as his sole task to pursue his own thoughts and find the right words to express them. He practiced a profession of which his readers were largely ignorant. They probably believed that words popped into a successful writer's head as readily as dividends flowed into a successful speculator's bank account.

His real life did not unfold in dining rooms or drawing rooms, but on the sheets of paper on his desk. Anything else was of only marginal interest to him, either as a pastime or, better still, as a literary stimulus. Only attractions of an exceptional nature could cause him to listen or look up. That such attractions existed, only those closest to him knew: his wife, his daughter, and possibly Frau Moser.

Klinger regarded it as his true if not exclusive purpose to find words for things and situations that had, he knew, been described innumerable times by other authors from the most diverse cultures. The very fact that he was determined to rename the old and eternally similar took up nearly all his time—his time at his desk, compared to which the time he spent in hotel dining rooms was wholly unimportant. It was, however, relaxing and, above all, profitable because he used it to observe the most trivial incidents that completely escaped other people, who noticed at most that he looked abstracted, which he wasn't. No one could have concentrated harder at such moments than Klinger. Although he seemed self-absorbed, he was really observing and analyzing those around him.

What he wrote had to bear comparison with the writings of his acknowledged and unacknowledged literary exemplars, which was why the time he spent at his desk was the most important time of all. It was possible to restate in another way what had already been written, because different words shed new light on what everyone saw or failed to see. Of course, what he felt he had to say didn't really need saying again. Although the world would continue to revolve if it remained unsaid, nothing could deter him from trying to say it. That was his mission, his daily occupation, his struggle: finding the right words. Nothing could be harder, and if he failed to find the right words he was sometimes forced to abandon scenarios that were already clearly mapped out in his mind's eye. The result of such reluctant demolition work was that many subsidiary characters fell by the wayside. That could happen, but that was also how he came to evolve other characters: through the intimate medium of the words he used to describe them and make them say and do things of which similar individuals in similar real-life situations might have been quite incapable.

Klinger liked to describe himself as a literary character without ever defining exactly what he meant by that. Whether and to what extent he exploited those around him for literary purposes, no one except his wife could probably have said. But his wife never discussed him with strangers on principle, and the forty-eight-year-old author shunned would-be biographers. So Klinger remained largely a mystery, which suited him perfectly. Everything about him was literature, as he put it. He was forever in search of the *mot juste*, forever trying to avoid even the most latent platitude, for if there was anything his work couldn't tolerate, it was empty words and phrases, which he regarded—and described—as "prejudices in wrapping paper." He could pontificate on this subject for hours and ruthlessly did so in the family circle. There he had no need to mince his words, no need to interrupt his flow for courtesy's sake or fear interruption from others. There he could say anything, and anything naturally entailed repeating himself. There he had no need to fear making a fool of himself. He talked and the others listened. Their attention might stray, but that didn't worry him. By talking he sometimes hit on other ideas, which was the main thing. What Marianne Klinger thought about this remained a secret from the outside world.

Usually, however, he sat at his desk, weighing one word against another. It could be a long time, hours or even days, before he was satisfied with his choice, and when he was he experienced feelings of unadulterated bliss. Because that didn't happen every day, or even every week, his consequent ill humor was known and dreaded by those closest to him, his wife and his children, who had long feared nothing in the world so much as their famous father's moods. But their fear of him had also taught them not to be afraid of anything else because, compared to Klinger's moods, anything else was innocuous.

———

At first Erneste took them for what they also were, of course: two quite unexceptional guests. A newlywed couple on their way to Italy, they were spending a few days beside the Lake of Brienz because many people regarded a stay in the Swiss Alps as essential a part of a honeymooner's itinerary as a visit to Venice. If Erneste noticed anything about these newlyweds, it was that they bore a startling resemblance to each other—indeed, they looked so alike they might easily have passed for brother and sister had it not been for their newly acquired marital status and the purpose of their trip. In other respects they were indistinguishable from the big batch of guests who checked in the same afternoon, three days after Klinger's arrival. There was no reason why the young couple should have attracted any more attention than the day's other new arrivals.

Erneste was supervising the transfer of luggage from the steamer to the cable car and up to the hotel, so he had little time to pay more than the requisite attention to individual guests. He hurried his assistants along and reassured anyone who had mislaid pieces of luggage.

Three days after her arrival in Giessbach, Erneste ran into Madame Jolivay, as the young woman who bore such a resemblance to her husband was called, in the corridor outside her room on the second floor. She was alone and dressed for going out, with a peacock feather in her hat. Was it chance, or had she contrived this encounter? Erneste had seen her in the interim, but only at a distance, and they hadn't exchanged a word before. It was Madame Jolivay who seized the opportunity to accost him.

She asked his name. It had scarcely escaped his lips when she cried: *"C'est toi, je n'ai pas tort! Erneste, mon petit Erneste! Ärnschdli! C'est toi! Dü bisch es!"* At that moment, of course, he recognized her, his cousin Julie from Erstein. In defiance of all the conventions he embraced her in the middle of the dimly lit corridor, in which no other guest or member of staff could be seen. The two cousins hugged each other like a pair of lovers after a long separation, and they remained in that position until Julie gently pushed him away and scrutinized him more closely. She screwed up her eyes and put out her right hand to touch his shoulder, then slowly let it fall. Erneste followed the gentle movement with his gaze.

"Julie, Julie," he said, "how long is it since we saw each other last?" And Julie said, "A long time. Ten years? No, it must be even longer!" They weren't speaking French now, of course. Being as drunk on memories as they were, they had lapsed into Alsatian German, the language they'd spoken together as children, which Erneste had never forgotten.

Erneste hadn't seen Julie since he was eleven, because that was when she and her parents had moved from

Strasbourg to Paris. In spite of her promise to write to him and think of him and see him every summer when they came back on vacation, she had never returned to the village because things didn't work out that way. Her parents had employed a notary to sell the house they owned in Erneste's native village, so they never visited Erstein again. All that Erneste ever received from Julie after the move to Paris, where her father, an engineer, had landed a job he'd been after for ages, were two or three postcards that anyone could read including the postmistress, the mailman, and his parents and brothers and sisters.

The woman he embraced in the corridor had grown up. She bore no resemblance to his little cousin of years ago. Her blue eyes were still the same, but that was all. If she hadn't accosted him he wouldn't have recognized her, because she was every inch an elegant Parisienne who smelled fragrantly of face powder and wore a *grain de beauté* on her left cheek, not a rumbustious girl who imitated her elders. No, he hadn't thought of Julie for ages. His memory of her had gradually faded like that of the village in which he had grown up and been unhappy, leaving behind a residue that dissipated as soon as he tried to grasp it. He had no wish to grasp it, either, because Erstein was as unimportant to him as if it had never existed. He wouldn't have recognized Julie by her voice or her walk. By her eyes, perhaps? Not knowing what it was about himself that had caused her to recognize him, he forbore to ask.

On the evening of the same day Julie introduced him to Philippe, her husband, who was interested solely in the design and manufacture of toys and board games, card games and construction sets, for which he had developed a boyhood passion that obviously meant more to him than anything and anyone else, even a new wife. Julie had known what she was letting herself in for when she married him three weeks earlier. Philippe saw marriage as a board game complete with live pieces, rules and penalties, winners and losers. Today's loser could be tomorrow's winner. He was blind to any infractions of the rules that occurred off the board because he never left it. To Julie marriage represented an opportunity—the only one she found acceptable—to gain her independence. To Philippe Jolivay it meant an opportunity to acquire a ready-made audience. He wanted children and she knew it.

Twenty-six years old, Philippe had for months been tirelessly engaged in constructing a new factory of his own outside Paris, a modern production facility in which he intended to put into practice all the ideas he had dreamed of since his boyhood.

His meeting with Erneste in the hotel lobby didn't take long: he stood up and shook hands, nodded and said a word or two. The *chef de réception* peered suspiciously in their direction. Protracted conversations between employees and guests disrupted the subtle social equilibrium. It was restored, however, when Philippe flopped back into his armchair, opened his notebook, picked up a pencil, and returned to his diagrams and calculations. It seemed that Julie's husband had something of an aversion to being distracted. All that interested him, Julie said as she sat down beside him, were "toys and games, toys and games. And now, Erneste, please bring us some nice, chilled white wine." Erneste was relieved to be able to withdraw and do as he was asked.

Philippe, he learned later, had been able to carry out his plans only because he'd inherited a substantial fortune a year before his marriage. "What was I supposed to do," Julie told Erneste, "marry a pauper? No, no, I always knew he'd be rich someday." Julie's contribution to the fulfillment of Philippe's dreams was to leave her husband in peace and lend her name to his factory at Vincennes. His firm, *Juliejouets*, which had maintained a satisfactory turn-over during World War II and achieved unforeseen successes thereafter, kept Philippe and his family well provided for. As for Julie, she bore him two daughters and two sons over the years.

Because Philippe and Julie were so seldom on the same wavelength, it was inevitable that the inevitable would happen and that, when it did, he noticed nothing. Dissatisfied with Philippe, Julie deserted the board and, at a stroke, invalidated the unwritten but universally familiar rules of the marital game on which she had embarked by saying "I do." This she did at Giessbach by committing her first and soon-to-be-repeated transgression, commonly known as adultery, under the noses of her unsuspecting husband and her cousin Erneste.

What rendered the affair even more hectic was that Julie's parting from her lover was as foreseeable as the affair itself had been. The prospect of saying goodbye was painful, but nothing could better allay the pain than to reopen the smarting wound at every opportunity. Erneste, who was initiated into the liaison, helped as best he could. He became the secret messenger responsible for exchanges of billets-doux between Julie and her English lover, Steve Boulton, just as he had been in other cases, for clandestine affairs were far from unusual at the Grand. A vacation fling like this one, in which no holds were barred provided you didn't get caught, was as routine there as at any other big hotel.

While Jakob concentrated on Klinger and his family, Erneste became more and more involved with Julie and Boulton, so it was only natural that at night, when they had finished work, they found plenty to tell each other about the people they waited on and had dealings with.

Boulton, who was on vacation without his family for the first time ever, already had two children, whereas Julie's first child, a girl, was born exactly nine months later. She was christened Victoria. Not Victorine or Victorienne, but Victoria—like the English queen, Julie liked to point out. She even, quite unnecessarily, drew attention to the fact that Victoria looked nothing like her or her husband, which seemed odd, given that Julie and Philippe might have been mistaken for brother and sister. Later, when her features gradually developed, the girl turned out to be the spitting image of Steve.

If someone had asked Philippe Jolivay whether he remembered a Mr Boulton he would merely have shaken his head, never having been introduced to the gentleman in question, but no one ever did. The truth was, as Julie often recalled with a girlish frisson, that their paths had probably crossed more than once in the dining room of Giessbach's Grand Hotel in 1936. She enjoyed recalling this. Her affair, she told herself, couldn't be over yet.

———•———

The affair between Erneste's cousin Julie and Steve Boulton, the London businessman, was far from over, in fact it seemed likely to endure for the rest of their days. In 1937, the year after they first met, they resumed their clandestine liaison, which they had maintained by letter in the meantime, and continued to do so regularly up to the outbreak of war. Until then their relationship was re-newed every summer at the Grand, in the immediate vicinity of their unwitting spouses and children. After the war, when the Grand was ruled out as a rendezvous because it had closed down in the interim, the lovers had to devise a convincing pretext for deserting their respec-tive families in London and Paris for at least three weeks every summer. Boulton officially devoted that period to an extended business trip on the Continent, mainly in Ger-man Switzerland, whereas Julie ostensibly stayed at a Swiss spa named Zurzach, where she took the waters for her arthritis. There was no reason to doubt their bona fides. Even when their relationship had long ceased to be an escapade, having become almost a habit, the need to keep it a secret from Philippe Jolivay and Angie Boulton still lent it a clandestine flavor. So Julie and Steve went on meeting at a small hotel farther along the lake, where they had no need to fear discovery as they had at Giessbach. No one there had a right to suspect them, still less spy on them. Although they were getting on in years, they long persisted in feeling like young lovers, at least during their secret assignations. It wasn't until the early 1960s that a certain constraint made itself felt when they were reunited, because no one could have failed to notice the gradual development of Steve's paunch and Julie's crow's-feet.

The mineral baths at Zurzach and the business trips to Switzerland were effective remedies for marital and professional tedium. Although Julie had paid only one visit to Zurzach, Steve really did do some traveling on business in Switzerland, so not all they told their spouses was fictitious.

9

Erneste got up at nine the next day. He dressed, looked in his wardrobe for a woolen cap, put it on, pulled it down over his eyes, and left the apartment to report in sick. The phone booth was on the other side of the street around a hundred yards from his door. To the surprise of all who knew him, Erneste would fail to turn up for work for the very first time.

He found it as much of an effort to call in sick as he had to get up and dress. His body felt empty—empty but unbearably cumbersome. It seemed to be reverberating from the blows it had sustained last night. He could hardly move, but he contrived to do so in the end, albeit slowly and with an immense effort. He managed to stand up and get dressed, swayed but didn't fall, put on his cap and went downstairs, crossed the street. His injuries didn't prevent him from phoning, and it struck him while he was doing so that he didn't think of last night as long as he was occupied. His cut lip split open and started to bleed while he was speaking, but no one saw it. No one could be allowed to see what a mess they'd made of him, and because the street was almost deserted at that hour and he was shielded from any inquisitive glances by the woolen cap, which he'd pulled down low over his eyes, no one did see him. He didn't call Julie. He had to work out what to do next. He'd known he had to do something ever since he woke up. His first thought had been of Jakob, his second of Klinger, with whom he had to get in touch. The only thing was, he didn't know how to go about it. Should he write to him, call him, or pay him a surprise visit at his home? He needed time to think. Well, now he had a whole day in which to think, and if necessary the night and the following day as well. That should be time enough.

He couldn't inflict his appearance on the patrons of the Restaurant am Berg—it was all too obvious what had happened to him—so he would stay away for the next few days. He told the manager he'd had a bad fall and might need hospital treatment. "Will you be all right?" he was asked. "Yes," he said, "I'll be fine."

He felt almost grateful to those thugs for confining him to his apartment. He would never have come to a definite decision at work, so now he could work things out at home. He had the time now. He must make the most of it, not fritter it away.

Last night, which seemed an eternity ago, Erneste had showered for minutes on end and then spent hours lying in a hot tub. To maintain the temperature as the water cooled, he let it run out and topped it up again and again because he had to erect a barrier against the chill that menaced him from within, which seemed to cool the water more quickly than usual.

And now he was lying open-eyed on his bed, trying to think. He wanted to straighten things out in his mind, but he still couldn't get to grips with them. He only dimly remembered getting home. He didn't recall how long it took or which way he had come. His vision was obscured by his swollen, blood-encrusted eyelids, so he might well have taken an hour to reach his apartment.

Regardless of the tenant who lived beneath him, he'd stretched out in the bath. To deaden the sound a little he put a washcloth under the spout, then filled the tub to the brim. No one had complained. He hadn't disturbed anyone, it seemed. The other occupants of the building slept on as he bathed, trying to wash off and forget what had happened. He knew he wouldn't succeed unless he did the right thing later. One bath wasn't enough, nor was a second.

After telephoning he went home again, undressed and got back into bed. Staring at the ceiling, he suddenly felt cold. He got up, shivering, and fetched a woolen blanket from the wardrobe, the only wardrobe he possessed, the one in which he kept his clothes, his underclothes and shirts, his bedsheets, his socks, his handkerchiefs, a few dog-eared magazines, a few letters, some writing materials, and a far too heavy suitcase. He'd spotted the wardrobe in the window of a junk shop and bought it only because the dealer had agreed to deliver it free of charge. That was ten years ago, and the wardrobe had cost him less than 50 francs. For ten years it had steadfastly remained in its place. Once the dealer had delivered and reassembled it, and once Erneste had filled it with all the objects that had lain scattered around his little apartment, he'd felt convinced that this innovation would change his life as well: no wardrobe, old life; new wardrobe, new life. Nonsensical though it was, that idea had haunted him for days until he finally had to acknowledge the obvious truth: nothing in his life would change for as long as he remained in this town and this apartment, with or without a new wardrobe and with or without the unaccustomed neatness that reigned in his home by virtue of this new piece of furniture. Nothing would change for as long as he didn't do something, but what? Now he *could* do something, and that would doubtless bring about a lot of changes.

The wardrobe was sheathed in white plastic. It was cheap and unsightly, and although it belonged to Erneste he hated looking at it, but he couldn't help doing so when he lay in bed because the bed was directly opposite. He disliked the wardrobe's pale, smooth expanse, so he always left one of the two doors open. This meant that he looked, not at the wardrobe itself, but at his clothes and the shelves and the darkness beyond them. The back wall of the wardrobe could not be seen. No one apart from him had ever seen the wardrobe in daylight because no one apart from him ever entered his bedroom during the day.

He lay down again, pulled up the bedclothes, and reviewed what had happened in the last few weeks. Nothing had happened, really, except that he had received first one letter and then another, and that each of those letters had stripped off a few more layers of scar tissue. Outwardly he was calm, but an explosion had taken place inside him, and the things it had dislodged were forcing their way to the surface. He was as conscious of this as he was of the cuts and bruises on his face. He knew what had happened, but he still didn't know what its sequel would be.

The next day his cuts began to heal and he felt better. At ten that morning he called the restaurant manager and informed him that he would be able to return to work on Tuesday next, possibly even on Monday. The manager no longer sounded concerned, in fact he seemed almost to have forgotten their conversation of the previous day. Erneste had to suppress a sneaking but quite unfounded fear that he might be fired because of his absence.

Then he called Julie at her small hotel. She was horrified when she heard what had happened, but he didn't spare her. He gave her a detailed account of what had occurred two nights before, shortly after they'd parted. She suggested coming to see him, but he declined the offer. He had to think things over, he said. "What things?" she asked, and wanted to know why he hadn't gone to the police and reported the incident. He merely said, "Enjoy your last day with Steve. I'll be all right. I'll write you if I've anything to write about, that's a promise. Write to me too."

She would be going back to Paris the next day. There was no good reason to repeat the farewells they'd already said two days ago. Julie never invited Erneste to visit her at home in France. When her happy days in Switzerland were over, she resumed her family life in Paris, which was only a little less happy than her secret life, just as Steve did in London.

"We'll see each other again next year," Erneste said. "Take good care of yourself," Julie replied after a brief pause. Those words brought uninvited tears to his eyes so suddenly, he couldn't restrain them. Fortunately, however, their conversation was at an end and he quickly pulled himself together. After a last goodbye he hung up, but he didn't leave the phone booth yet.

He was out of reach. No one knew where he was and no one could call him, but he could call anyone he chose. If someone had been waiting outside the booth he might have had second thoughts, but no one was, so he had no reason to change his mind. It all seemed quite straightforward. He couldn't put it off any longer.

Klinger lived in a small village farther along the lake. What had become of his children? Why should he care? They'd probably remained behind in the States. The magazines Erneste read at the hairdresser's had never mentioned them, only Klinger's wife, and only because she'd died a few weeks before the article was published. As luck would have it, the name of the village where Julius Klinger lived had lodged in his memory.

It didn't take him long to find Klinger's number in the phone book, which looked as if it had never been used. He inserted twenty centimes and proceeded to dial it. Miraculously, his hands had been spared. Five rings, then a woman's voice, possibly the daughter. No, a domestic servant. "Klinger residence," she said. "How may I help you?"

Erneste said his name, but it meant nothing to her. She inquired his reason for wanting to speak with Klinger. "A personal matter," Erneste replied. "It's urgent."

"Urgent?"

"Yes, it's most important I speak with him right away."

"Impossible, I'm afraid. He never takes calls in the mornings, not from anyone. What's it about?"

"I can't explain over the phone."

"I'm sorry, then I can't put you through. If I'm to put you through I'll have to know what it's about. Are you a journalist? A writer?"

"It's to do with a mutual acquaintance."

"Who, exactly?"

"If he hears who it is he may not want to speak with me at all."

"In that case, I'm sure he'll have his reasons."

"But I have to speak with him."

"Then tell me what it's about."

Belatedly, Erneste searched around for some pretext. But he couldn't think of a pretext or a lie, so he told the truth: "Tell him it's about Jakob. He knows him."

"Jakob? Jakob Meier?" the woman said after a pause. There was another silence before she asked, "What's happened?"

"I can't tell you that, I need to speak with Herr Klinger personally. Jakob Meier has written to me—he's written to me twice. Have a word with Herr Klinger, tell him I must speak with him. Tell him I've had some news from Jakob. It isn't good."

There was evidently no need for her to consult with Klinger. "Come this afternoon," she said. "Herr Klinger will be able to spare you some time then. Come after two. Are you a friend of Jakob's?"

"I knew him well. As well as Klinger. Even better, perhaps."

"Really?" Her wry tone of voice conveyed that she had also made Jakob's acquaintance.

10

The old intimacy between Erneste and Jakob seemed to be returning little by little, and Erneste wondered if this might have something to do with the exceptionally hot weather. Giessbach, where lower temperatures were usually recorded than in Thun or Interlaken, had been swelteringly hot since the middle of July. In the Grand Hotel's guests, this heat engendered a state of torpid indifference to themselves, other people and world events. No matter what happened, the heat held sway. During the day, at least, it blurred and obliterated everything that was normally well defined and firmly established.

People didn't start to bestir themselves until dusk, when the sun had gone down at last and the air was somewhat cooler, and when they bestirred themselves they experienced a vague revulsion for the inactivity to which they had so utterly surrendered throughout the day. But Mother Nature proved irresistible. For all their good intentions, they found themselves constrained to further inactivity between dusk and the following morning. "It's like the Tropics," said those who could be assumed to know what they were talking about, having traveled widely. "Far too hot to think," said others.

Since most of the guests retired to their darkened bedrooms after lunch or took the cable car down to the lake for a swim, the work of the staff was also affected by the unaccustomed temperatures. Their services were in less demand than usual, especially in the afternoons, so they were granted some additional hours off. This gave Erneste more time to devote to Julie, whereas Jakob caught up on his sleep or read.

Certain of the guests had taken to dressing lightly in the mornings and strolling to the Giessbach Falls, there to be bedewed with spray by the mighty cascades. Having succeeded in shaking off their almost insuperable torpor, at least for a few minutes, these walkers could look forward to a little refreshment after their exertions. Although they set off back to the hotel feeling reinvigorated, their respite from the heat was short-lived. Many divested themselves of unwelcome articles of clothing in the course of their brief perambulations, but none was immodest enough to transgress the bounds of decorum. Any liberties they took remained within acceptable limits.

But a steadily dwindling minority, to which Julius Klinger belonged, rigidly observed the dress code. Despite the inordinate heat, men like him never appeared in public other than in a white shirt and a dark, three-piece suit with all the buttons done up. Moist-browed and smelling faintly of cologne, Klinger thereby advertised his affinity with the celebrated Mayor of New York who never left his house unaccompanied by a manservant bearing a flatiron with which, if need arose, to rid his master's jacket of undesirable creases. Unlike his wife, and certainly in contrast to his children, Klinger considered slovenliness in matters of dress to be an inexcusable breach of propriety, though he never tried to impose his views on his family.

Although no more lax than usual, morals were rather more liberally interpreted because of the heat. Thoroughgoing immorality of the kind practiced by Julie and her lover persisted in secret. The Grand's walls had no ears and its staff were models of discretion. The more people complained of the heat, the more thoroughly they could enjoy it. They surrendered to it by lolling or lying in sunbleached loungers shaded by the tremulous foliage of ancient trees, drowsing or reading. Now and then their arms would sag and their books and newspapers fall to the grass as they dozed off, only to awake feeling bemused after lying too long in the full glare of the sun, which had moved in the interim.

Any guests who were hungry repaired to the dining room for lunch. It was slightly cooler in there than outside because fans had been installed in all four corners of the room, causing clothes and curtains to billow in the artificial draft created by their humming electric motors. Only a small minority persisted in lunching on the terrace, their sole protection the sun umbrellas beneath which ice cubes swiftly melted and cold cuts acquired an unappetizing appearance, so the speed with which they had to eat and drink soon generated a convivial atmosphere. Klinger's children were among those who patently enjoyed the lunchtime inferno. Josefa in silk blouses and Maximilian in open-necked, short-sleeved shirts, both wearing sandals or sometimes even barefoot, they quickly became the focal point and nucleus of a small, heat-resistant coterie whose membership varied from day to day.

Erneste was able to watch them from his post inside the dining room, where he could see and hear them laughing, and he noticed that the young Klingers never lacked for company, not always of their own age. They were a genuine attraction: young and seemingly carefree, good-looking, dreamy and romantic but also a trifle lost. The world was still their unopened oyster. Out on the terrace they were served by a Sicilian waiter who found the heat easier to contend with than his colleagues. Back in the dining room he sometimes recounted what went on outside: nothing of importance, just youthful fun, the boy still little more than a child, the girl besieged by admirers. It was she who did most of the talking, but the Germans spoke too fast for the Sicilian to understand much of what was said.

Peace descended when lunch was over. A child cried, a falcon described tight spirals in the sky, another described wider spirals below it, a crow launched itself between them, cawing loudly, clouds veiled the sun and drifted away, the only hoped-for rain in July was one violent downpour during the night, the air smelled of marjoram and eucalyptus, of indigenous herbs and others that didn't grow there—or perhaps they did. Everyone, even those who had lunched on the terrace under sun umbrellas, disappeared by two o'clock at the latest. The waiters were the last to leave the dining room after clearing away and setting the tables afresh. Work proceeded unremittingly but in silence behind the reception desk. Herr Direktor Wagner's bowed figure emerged from his office now and then. He straightened up only when guests approached; as soon as they were gone he subsided once more. The silence was broken only by the unsuppressible ringing of the telephone, the distant cries of a child, the high-pitched scream of a bird of prey, the harsh cawing of a crow, the voice of the receptionist picking up the phone or putting it down. The conversations he conducted didn't last long as a rule. The callers were nearly always put through to the rooms upstairs, most of which had phones of their own—a rare prewar luxury in this remote part of the world. Sometimes guests ordered water, lemonade, or ice. The receptionist would then pass a brief message to the room waiter on duty in the kitchen, who was poised to receive orders and jumped up from his chair whenever the phone rang. Grateful for any interruption, the room waiter fetched what was required and carried it upstairs on a tray. And so the unwontedly long afternoons crept by in an atmosphere of unwonted lethargy. What had to be done was done with as little mental exertion as possible.

Because Jakob's work in the hotel bar could keep him up until dawn, he did not have to wait table in the middle of the day. By the time he went to bed he had exceeded regulation working hours by such a margin that he could sleep for as long as he wanted. His services weren't required until four. The bar opened at six.

Jakob would still be asleep when Erneste got up in the mornings, having seldom gone to bed before three. The temperature scarcely fell at night, so they slept in the nude. Erneste's excitement mounted with every breath, with every breath of his own and of Jakob's, with every thought and every twitch of Jakob's fingers. It wasn't easy to resist the sight of his friend asleep, and Erneste felt no shame when he masturbated beside him.

Erneste got up and sluiced himself at the washbasin. The intimacy prevailing between the two young men seemed to have reached a ne plus ultra. Erneste had the feeling that Jakob belonged to him, or if not Jakob, then his body, just as his own body belonged to Jakob. His life had completely changed since the first day they met.

Jakob entered their room so quietly in the small hours that Erneste seldom heard him come in. When he did hear him, however, he was wide awake in an instant. He could identify each piece of clothing as it fell to the floor. Jacket, vest, shirt, trousers, underpants, socks—his state of arousal became more intense with every discarded garment.

He didn't pull away when Jakob stretched out beside him and put his hand on his shoulder. On the contrary, he did whatever Jakob wanted, and with passionate alacrity. Instantly overcome by the same desire, he always grasped what Jakob required of him, undeterred even by the odors with which his friend's skin had lately been impregnated, for at night he smelled of tobacco smoke and sometimes of drink, though he himself didn't drink, he claimed, and Erneste didn't doubt this. So the smells of the hotel bar condensed and mingled with the cooking smells that assailed Erneste whenever he entered the hotel kitchen, suffusing his own skin to such an extent that they were hard to wash off. Also evoked by their sweat and their kisses were the multifarious sounds of the day, the chefs' brusque voices, their colleagues' bustling footsteps, the guests' unintelligible chatter. All these clung to their skin like a film at the end of one working day and the start of the next—together, no doubt, with the fears and misgivings of which guests never spoke, no matter how evident they were.

Jakob sometimes woke up while Erneste was getting dressed. Then all it took was a twitch of the hand, a glance, a single bat of the eyelid, for Erneste to join him on the bed. Often, however, Jakob was so sound asleep that Erneste could watch him at his leisure. There were times when Jakob's eyelids quivered as his eyes moved beneath them and he clenched his fists and lashed out at some invisible adversary. Erneste never discovered who it was because they didn't talk about their dreams. Then Jakob would quieten again and lie there with his teeth just visible between his slightly parted lips, as handsome and almost inviolable as if he were remote from everything, even from himself, and Erneste had to turn away.

There were reasons enough to mistrust the future—indeed, to dread it. This war everyone was talking about—how ineluctably terrible it would be once it started, rending everything and everyone apart. Although it was all Erneste could do not to wake Jakob up, he let him sleep on. Erneste, too, felt convinced that war was inevitable. They couldn't possibly be wrong, all these people who were so much better informed than himself. They all talked about the war, and if they didn't talk about it they thought about it, you could tell that just by looking at them.

When Erneste came back to the room after lunch, Jakob was usually still in bed, sleeping, reading, or bookkeeping. He had a little cashbook in which he kept a record of his income and outgoings, and he was understandably pleased when the former exceeded the latter. He engaged in this bookkeeping as often as he could. "I'm going to be rich someday," he said once. Erneste didn't feel any pride or respect when Jakob said such things, just a mixture of compassion and uneasiness. He felt tempted to say, "No, you'll never be rich, neither of us will, we don't have what it takes." But because hurting Jakob was the last thing he wanted to do, and because he considered Jakob vulnerable, he said nothing and hoped his silence would be eloquent. But Jakob didn't get the message. Erneste should have been more explicit, he should have told him point-blank that success was reserved for other people. Jakob inhabited a wider world than Erneste. He possessed a confidence that Erneste lacked, and it may have been this confidence that made him so strong. Jakob's ideas transcended his present circumstances.

Because the heat in the attic room was almost unbearable during the day, Jakob used to swathe himself in a damp towel. Cocooned in this, he would lie on the bed and sleep, pursue his extravagant daydreams, or do his sums. Quite often, too, he would read and fall asleep while reading. And so, when Erneste entered their room after lunch, he would find him either asleep, or daydreaming, or figuring, or reading. Although Jakob was making only slow progress with the big book he was reading, he didn't give up but pressed on undaunted. Several minutes could go by before he tackled the next page of Klinger's *Oporta*, but he refused to be beaten, intent on plumbing the big book's secrets. And because he gave Erneste an almost daily résumé of what he'd read, Erneste ended by knowing at least the first chapter of that much-lauded, widely read masterpiece almost as well as if he'd read it himself.

It wasn't long before the towel began to dry off. Jakob would then get up, dump it in the washbasin, run cold water over it, wring it out, wrap it around himself and lie down again. "That's better," he would say, looking up at Erneste. And Erneste would get undressed, cup his hands under the faucet, sluice himself down at the washbasin and hold his head under the running water. Then everything would be damp: the sheets and his body, first cool, then tepid, and before long the room beneath the eaves would begin to steam like a paradisal dungeon with locks and keys to which the outside world had no access. Erneste would lie down beside Jakob, the hush broken only by the occasional creak of a beam above the thin attic ceiling as the heat brought the timber back to life.

Erneste felt best of all when they lay silently side by side, when no words were needed and any word would only have broken the spell. He disliked it intensely when Jakob made disparaging remarks about some guest, which sadly happened more and more often. "You've no right to speak that way," he would tell him sternly. "Not about someone who helps to provide your bread and butter." But his rebukes fell on deaf ears. Jakob merely laughed at him, and his laughter was infectious. "Bread and butter, bread and butter!" he scoffed, imitating Erneste's Alsatian accent, and in the end Erneste laughed too.

Erneste couldn't shake off the suspicion that Jakob's opinions of certain guests weren't really his own, and that he'd picked them up from someone else. Some of their fellow employees were always gossiping about the guests. "I'm not interested," Erneste would say. "It's no business of mine. We aren't like them and they aren't like us. As long as they let us get on with our work we shouldn't concern ourselves with them. If they find fault with us, they probably have good reason to." But usually he said little when Jakob inveighed against German philistines and avaricious Jews. "How do you know?" he would retort. "You can't possibly know about such things." Alternatively, he would let Jakob talk until he ran out of ideas.

One day Erneste came across a 5-franc piece under Jakob's pillow. When he asked him how the freshly minted coin had gotten there—it was dated 1936— and why he hadn't put it away with the rest of his savings, Jakob hesitated briefly. His hesitation aroused Erneste's suspicions, and Erneste's raised eyebrows made Jakob waver. The money was Jakob's, of that he had no doubt: it was under his pillow and Erneste hadn't missed any money. Jakob hesitated, but then he opened his hand and Erneste dropped the coin into it, a small addition to the slowly growing nest egg with which Jakob hoped to secure his future after the war, if war actually came: a small hotel in Cologne or a roadhouse beside the Rhine— something of the kind.

"How did the money get under your pillow?" Jakob couldn't remember at first. Then he did remember after all: it was a tip from a guest who had checked out a few days earlier. He said his name, and Erneste recalled the man in question. Five francs was a lot of money, but ever since Jakob had been working in the hotel bar his personal gratuities had been piling up. They were a reward for the obliging way he attended to his customers in the bar at night—customers who sat drinking until the small hours and would have resented it if a barman seemed eager to get rid of them. Jakob's face betrayed no such impatience. Having worries enough of their own, the refugees couldn't abide other people's. They may also have been purchasing his silence, for many of the émigrés stranded here had a dread of German informers. Were they afraid Jakob might be one?

Jakob was holding the coin in his fist. "It probably fell out of my pocket when I was getting undressed," he said. He kissed Erneste and stretched out on the bed with his arms behind his head. Erneste forgot all about his discovery. He was reminded of it eleven days later.

I I

Shortly after one o'clock he boarded the local train that ran along the lakeshore in an easterly direction. The journey took thirty-seven minutes. The car in which he was sitting was only sparsely occupied, for the most part by elderly folk and a few children. The train was on time. Passengers alighted at every station but none got in, so he had the car to himself after the fourth stop. The place where Klinger lived obviously wasn't a tourist resort, and the commuters who used the local train every day were at work. Erneste tried to concentrate on the scenery—lake on the left, little villages and vineyards on the right—but his thoughts were elsewhere. His eyes skimmed the unfamiliar countryside, most of which slid past him unnoticed. The individual stations left no lasting impression. On one occasion he was struck by the brownish foliage of some parched geraniums on the windowsill of a waiting room. Seated on the bench outside was a girl of around seventeen. She was looking infinitely bored—as neglected as the flowers behind her. Another time his window was lashed by a sudden rainstorm, but the sun reappeared within minutes. He registered this without surprise.

Erneste was wearing a pale-blue polka-dot tie with his gray suit, the only suit he possessed, which did for all occasions, and over it a light raincoat. His umbrella he'd wedged between the seat and the armrest. It fell over twice, and twice he wedged it back again. He tried hard to concentrate. It still wasn't too late to change his mind, but if he didn't change his mind he had to be well prepared. But that meant trying to imagine something that defied his imagination: a meeting with Klinger, face to face.

After thirty-seven minutes the train stopped for the sixth time. Erneste got out and the train continued on its way. He studied the timetable. Trains back to Giessbach left every hour.

He needed a drink before he set off for Klinger's place, so he walked past the ticket office and into the little station restaurant. He was feeling weak. His hands were trembling, but he knew how to cure this. He had time for a brandy.

He pushed open the heavy glass door, the handle of which was sticky to the touch. The airless room contained a sprinkling of eating, drinking, smoking lunchtime customers, each of whom was contributing to the stale and stuffy atmosphere. An elderly woman with unwashed gray hair looked up as Erneste came in and eyed him over the top of her glasses. The waitress looked half asleep, but she was quick off the mark. Three minutes later he was sitting in front of a lukewarm, leathery-tasting *cognac maison*. The little tray was adorned with a complimentary "dead man's leg", one of those rock-hard hazelnut cookies the locals liked so much. Erneste picked up his glass and drained it at a gulp, then paid and left. He hadn't removed his raincoat. None of the Restaurant am Berg's patrons would have recognized him in this setting, nor, in all probability, would he have recognized them—if any had strayed here, which was most unlikely.

Qu'il était beau, le Postillon de Longjumeau . . .

The melody had been going around and around in his head ever since he emerged from the restaurant. There was no cab rank, and it appeared from the bus-stop signboard that buses drove straight along the lake to the next village without halting en route. And so, rather irresolutely, he set off inland, hoping to meet someone he could ask for directions. His gamble paid off. Before long he met a man walking a big black dog. Not only was the man able to direct him, but the equanimity with which he did so conveyed that it certainly wasn't the first time he'd been asked the same question. The locals must be used to strangers asking them the way to Klinger's house, Erneste reflected. Everyone here must know who he is and where he lives.

The man asked Erneste if he was a journalist, but it was courtesy, not curiosity, that prompted the question. Erneste said he wasn't. "There aren't any taxis here," the man said. Erneste said he hadn't expected there to be any and would walk. "You can't go wrong," the man said. "The village is small—you can't miss it. Carry on up the hill, turn right after three or four hundred yards, then straight uphill again and make another right. You'll see, you get the finest view of the lake and the mountains from there." That terminated the conversation, and Erneste set off again.

Perhaps the man was a little curious after all, he told himself. He thought he could sense his eyes on his back, but he didn't turn around. Perhaps he was mistaken. The dog, which hadn't made a sound before, emitted a hoarse bark, but not at him. Perhaps the man had encountered someone else walking a dog, but that wasn't his concern.

Qu'il était beau, le Postillon de Longjumeau . . .

A quarter of an hour later he was standing outside Klinger's gate. The house was almost obscured by a tall, dense yew hedge, so its size could only be guessed at. The gate was low enough, however, to reveal that a narrow path flanked by shrubs and rose bushes led up to the front door. Everything made an overgrown, neglected impression. The wilted roses had not been removed, the gate was coated with a thin film of lichen, and there was a tile lying smashed outside the front door, having presumably fallen from the roof of the porch. There was still time to turn around, and for a moment Erneste was tempted to do so. His failure to show up would probably pass unnoticed; Klinger must receive so many visitors that it would be of no consequence. Beyond this gate, beyond these unseen walls, lay a world in which he had no business and nothing to gain. He knew this as certainly as if he really knew that world, but he knew it only from the outside, as an observer, in his capacity as a waiter. Seen from the outside it possessed no appeal for him. If he rang the bell now, he would be doing it for Jakob. The only thing he could do for him was to try to speak with Klinger. Perhaps they would come to terms, perhaps not. Klinger was a famous man whose sole connection with Erneste was that he had blighted his insignificant life over thirty years earlier, or at least rendered his insignificant life a little more insignificant than it already was.

The bell was on the right of the gate. Erneste stared at the button and the brass plate engraved with Klinger's initials, which was weatherworn and tarnished. He'd been expecting a more impressive reception. He put out his hand and pressed the button three times. Before long a buzzer sounded, the gate gave a click and swung back a few inches. He pushed it open and walked up to the house. The front door opened.

He recognized the housekeeper who had joined the Klingers in the summer of 1936 and then accompanied them to America. Frau Moser stood in the doorway, waiting for him to climb the five steps that led up to the dilapidated porch. She greeted him in a low voice, her face expressionless, and he got the feeling that she never raised her voice or registered any emotion. Although she wasn't wearing an apron, it was obvious that she wasn't a member of the family. The fact that she didn't introduce herself wasn't the only indication of her subordinate status.

Frau Moser stepped aside, took Erneste's coat, and asked him to wait in the anteroom. Then she withdrew, leaving him alone. She knows everything, he told himself, but she would never talk about it to anyone else. The door remained ajar. The house made a deserted but not unoccupied impression.

Erneste found himself standing in a room filled with books. It wasn't an anteroom, as Frau Moser had called it, but a library. In the center was a library table with two deep armchairs drawn up to it. The walls were lined with ceiling-high bookshelves, and between them stood display cabinets housing *objets* and mementos, gifts and souvenirs from distant lands. They included things Erneste had never seen before: Etruscan clasps, Chinese porcelain, Indian fabrics, pre-Columbian arrows, African figurines, Stone Age tools and countless fossils. Any space on the walls not occupied by books was given over to framed butterfly collections, *vedute*, drawings and sketches, copperplate engravings, a naked athlete, and copies of old masters. In one corner was a house plant whose pale-green tendrils brushed the ceiling and proliferated over the bookshelves.

The source of the curiously warm glow in which the room was bathed seemed natural, but it couldn't have been because the sun had gone in. Although the house looked rather rundown and depressing from the outside, what Erneste could see of the interior made a tranquil, cheerful impression. Every object and piece of furniture in this private paradise, from which the outside world had been banished, was of the finest quality. To have compared this paradise, even for a moment, with his own little apartment would have been inappropriate in the extreme, for everything in it defied comparison with anything he'd ever seen. So Jakob had spent a part of his life surrounded by beautiful objects like these—exactly how long, Erneste had no idea, and it occurred to him that Jakob and Klinger might have parted after only a short time. So what was Klinger supposed to pay Jakob for—what did he owe him? Like so many turns of phrase in Jakob's letters, the significance of that one—*He owes me, it's only right!*—still eluded him.

Klinger suddenly appeared in the doorway through which Erneste had entered the room a few minutes earlier. Since the door was ajar and Erneste was sitting with his back to it, Klinger took him by surprise—indeed, he startled him, and for an instant Erneste thought he'd done so on purpose. Klinger cleared his throat and Erneste jumped up. An invisible man had suddenly become visible, a rear view turned into a frontal view, a frozen image started to quiver. What it represented was unexpectedly coming to life. The scene that had etched itself into Erneste's memory on the afternoon of July 28, 1936, capable of being conjured up afresh at any time, often after an interval of years, became irrelevant for a few moments. Klinger had aged, that was unmistakable, but Erneste recognized him at once.

Equally unmistakable was the almost instantly suppressed dismay in Klinger's eyes at the sight of what remained of the treatment to which Erneste had been subjected a few days earlier: the traces of the savage beating that had prompted him to get in touch with Klinger after previously deciding, only a short while before, to let Jakob stew in his own juice and avoid all further thought of him. Klinger's deep-set eyes were in surprising contrast to the rest of his appearance. He had the impenetrably remote, self-absorbed look of an owl. His deliberately nonchalant manner failed to conceal the fact that he was on his guard.

He came over to Erneste. He was taller than Erneste remembered, and didn't look his age. He would be seventy-eight in a few weeks' time.

Then Klinger did something Erneste hadn't expected, although it was quite natural: he shook hands. He held Erneste's hand longer than necessary, looking him in the eye as if to gauge his sincerity. At that moment the image of Klinger that had poisoned his memory for so many years returned, and he involuntarily withdrew his hand, convinced that the other man must know what was going through his mind. Despite himself, he saw him again as he had seen him on that day in July of 1936, when he, Erneste, had made his unheralded appearance—when he had been inadvertently but all the more cruelly compelled to acknowledge that his hold over Jakob was no more, and that he had probably lost it a long time ago. Klinger possessed the power to dominate others, body and soul.

Even before they sat down at the table and Frau Moser came in with a laden tray, Klinger surprised Erneste by saying, "It's a long time ago, but I do remember you. You were Jakob's young friend. Ah well, we were all young once." The casual way he spoke conveyed that Erneste had played no great part in his memories of those days. All that surprised Erneste was that Klinger remembered him at all.

"You were a self-effacing young man—a perfect waiter. Better than Jakob ever was, discreet and . . . It might have been better if I'd taken you with me instead of him." Klinger fell silent while Frau Moser was putting the tray on the table. After she had gone he went on in the same tone: "Please help yourself to tea or coffee. Frau Moser baked the cake herself, she's an excellent cook. Frau Moser"—who was presumably waiting next door, ready to be summoned at any time—"is the only person I have left from the old days. Nearly everyone close to me is elsewhere or dead. My wife, my son—nearly everyone." Klinger never took his eyes off Erneste. "My daughter remained in the States. She has a family, in fact she's a grandmother herself."

Although he made a forthright impression, Erneste didn't feel bound to repay candor with candor. Later, perhaps, but not now. Did Klinger hope that his forthrightness would elicit confidences and help him to attain his goal as quickly as possible—was he simply interested in learning as much about Jakob as he could? Erneste was unentitled to ask questions of him and had no right to any answers, but he would dearly have liked to know why Klinger was being so communicative. The morose, exhausted old man of his expectations had turned out to be a person with a constitution of a sixty-year-old. Klinger was neither morose nor exhausted but talkative and clearly in good health. Erneste had the impression that the man he had come to ask something of was really asking something of him: the truth about Jakob. But what truth? Klinger wasn't to know that Erneste didn't know it himself. He knew as little of Jakob as Klinger, but at least he had news of him in the shape of two letters.

Klinger was used to determining how he spent his time, so it was only natural that he should also determine how those who took up his time should spend theirs, no matter what they wished to discuss with him. Although he didn't devote long to courtesies, he remained approachable—or at least, he did his utmost to create that impression. Erneste had little time left in which to think. He had no plan, so he abandoned the idea of proceeding methodically. He helped himself to some coffee and a slice of cake—it was too late to decline. He wasn't hungry, but he would finish the cake, every last morsel of it.

Klinger took neither tea nor coffee nor cake. He leaned back in his chair and sat there without moving for a while. Then, quite suddenly, his hand shot out with the forefinger leveled at Erneste. "Up there in the room that time—" he said. "It must have been awful for you." Erneste hadn't expected that either.

* * *

The scene that met his eyes on July 28, 1936, which was to imprint itself on his memory forever, was of two men in the following position: one standing with his legs apart, facing the door and the beholder, the other kneeling on the floor, so close to him that there could be no doubt what was going on. The older man was bending so low over the younger man, who could have been his son, that his forehead was almost touching his shoulder. The man crouching on the floor was naked, whereas the other man had removed only some of his clothing. One was Klinger, the other Jakob. Klinger was wearing gold cufflinks bearing his initials.

Because Erneste had opened the door carefully, as he always did when he assumed that Jakob was still asleep, it was several seconds before Klinger, and soon afterward Jakob, became aware that they were no longer alone. In Klinger's case, that happened at latest when Erneste closed the door softly but not inaudibly behind him. Although the stuffy little room was naturally filled with sounds of human origin, with noises of varied provenance and odors as well, every sound and odor had vanished from the scene Erneste would later see again and again. It was a silent, lifeless, almost monochrome picture.

Also visible in that picture was Klinger's jacket, which lay behind him and to one side. He, who set so much store by his outward appearance, had let it fall to the floor, and half on top of it, half in front of it, lay his vest. His shirt was half-unbuttoned down the front, and his undershirt, beneath which the shape of Jakob's left hand could be glimpsed, had ridden up. It was easy to guess what the other hand was holding.

A plump bluebottle was launching repeated assaults on the window pane, but Erneste was the only one who registered its futile attempts to escape. Lying on the unmade bed was Jakob's damp towel, the one he used to keep himself cool, and lying on that was a shiny new 5-franc piece, a reward for his contribution to Klinger's wellbeing. Erneste's right hand started to twitch at the sight of it. No one had been expecting him.

Being unusually tired that day, he had asked Monsieur Flamin for permission to knock off early, almost as if he'd had a presentiment of some kind. In fact, he was merely tired. He'd had no presentiment, because if he'd had the least suspicion he certainly wouldn't have acted on it.

It had been just two o'clock when he went upstairs, wanting to see Jakob and have a rest. Now he was standing behind Jakob and facing Klinger, a simple situation devoid of mystery.

Klinger had finished his lunch shortly before one as usual; Erneste had seen him leave. He had accompanied his wife to her room, then hurried off to see Jakob. His children were still out on the terrace.

He was cupping Jakob's head in both hands. His thumbs were pointing upward, his palms covering Jakob's ears and blotting out any distant sounds. Nothing could have made it plainer that Jakob's body, which Erneste had hitherto regarded as his property, was his no longer, yet it didn't matter in the least whether Jakob had sold his body or was placing it at Klinger's disposal for pleasure's sake. What Jakob was doing, he was doing of his own free will, not under any kind of compulsion. None of the arguments he might adduce to justify his behavior could change that. Jakob's body had ceased to belong to Erneste and his voice would no longer reach him. Jakob had passed into Klinger's possession.

Klinger straightened up. Whatever had prompted him to look up at that moment, an intake of breath or the absence of it, he now met Erneste's troubled gaze. Initial surprise gave way to a look of utter consternation. A member of the Grand Hotel's staff had caught the celebrated author, the husband and father of two children, being fellated in an attic like a male prostitute's john. There were more repugnant forms of illicit sexual intercourse between males, undoubtedly, but this one was embarrassing enough to bring the blood rushing to his cheeks.

It was only another two or three seconds before Jakob, too, grasped what had happened, because Klinger pushed him away. One glance at Klinger's face was enough: Jakob turned, saw Erneste standing where he had expected to see a closed door, and stared at him open-mouthed, a little saliva trickling down his chin. Klinger stooped and took hold of his waistband, which slipped through his fingers, then primly covered his nakedness.

Not a word was said as he hurriedly got dressed—not a word for as long as he was still present. Jakob, who made no move to rise and get dressed too, handed him his vest and jacket, picking them up in turn without taking his eyes off Erneste. Erneste stepped aside and opened the door, and Klinger went out without meeting his eye. For a while the door remained wide open. Klinger's hurried footsteps could be heard descending the stairs. Erneste and Jakob were alone together.

———•——

Klinger's supposition that Erneste must have been appalled by his discovery hung in the air, undisputed and unconfirmed. Erneste looked down at his slice of cake. He took a bite and drank some coffee, waiting because he knew that Klinger would go on without being prompted.

"Until that moment I knew nothing of your relationship with Jakob—he had never mentioned you. I was even unaware that he shared his room with someone, although I felt sure he'd already acquired a certain amount of experience in the relevant respect. In the big city, though, not in Giessbach. When you walked into that room, which I'd thought he occupied on his own, I naturally concluded that it was an error—that you'd mistaken the door or were an unknown roommate who was horrified by what met his eye because he'd never seen such a thing before. It wasn't until later that I grasped the truth of the matter. Jakob told me in America about the part you'd played in his life. An important part, he said, and I believed him. I would certainly have believed you too, but I seem to recall we didn't exchange a word, did we? Later I realized that the man who had caught us together, a faceless individual, was the impassive waiter who sometimes escorted us to our table in the dining room. But what would have been the point of trying to wean myself from Jakob? It was too late. I was besotted with him—I wouldn't have given him back to anyone."

Klinger spoke in a halting but resolute voice. He searched for the right words and seemed to know that they came easily to him as long as he had a listener, and Erneste was prepared to absorb every last detail Klinger confided in him. He spoke as if he had been waiting for this moment for decades.

"He often mentioned you later on, in America, but ours wasn't the kind of relationship that lent itself to intimate revelations or conversations. I won't pretend to you: he mentioned you to humiliate me, not out of nostalgia or love. I knew my young friend too well—I'd seen through him long ago—but that didn't quench my infatuation, my absolute readiness to make a fool of myself and remain dependent on him, or my devotion to his beauty—far from it. He knew me too—he knew me as a master knows his dog. He had no need to beat his dog. One look, one word sufficed and it came to heel—I came to heel. Jakob exploited his strength and my weakness to the full, and always to his own advantage. I was the ridiculous old man, he the glamorous youngster. He was handsome, and he knew how to make the most of his looks, in fact he even managed to enhance them as time went by. Knowing him, you'll understand what I mean, I'm sure. I still don't know how he did it, but his physical beauty seemed self-perpetuating. He was in possession of the drug I needed daily and couldn't dispense with. I was compelled to buy it from him because I couldn't live without it. So he kept me prisoner, titillating and exciting me until I had to possess him. Only then was I at peace—at peace and utterly at his mercy. But when he refused me I couldn't work. He starved me of oxygen. The snake lay basking in the Californian sunshine, replete and content, whereas the rabbit nearly expired of thirst.

"I'd devised a pretext for keeping him near me all the time: I managed to persuade him to learn to type. Because no one was allowed to disturb me while I was working, we spent hours alone together. No one took it amiss if I closeted myself with Jakob during the day. As my secretary, it was his duty to be available at all times. Nobody suspected anything. I enabled him to lead a comfortable life in my gradually shrinking shadow, and I enabled myself to delight in his constant presence. I was happy to be privileged to kiss and fondle him now and then. Occasionally he permitted me to do more than that. Meantime, he typed my manuscripts without understanding much of what he read—not a difficult job because my handwriting is legible. He also waited table at lunch and dinner. My wife insisted on that. "What a handsome boy he is," she used to say. "It's nice to have someone like him around." I liked to watch him on such occasions and see the pleasure his appearance inspired in other people, and sometimes he would give me a glance that epitomized our complicity. Then I felt proud—and yearned to kiss his hands in front of everyone, but I naturally restrained

myself. After dinner, if he didn't have to drive us anywhere, his time was his own. He had a room over the
garage, not that I ever entered it. He used to go out at
nights. I left him to his own devices and allowed him to
use the car, but I never asked him whom he met and what
he got up to. He picked up English quickly and made
himself popular, and how could I have reproached him for
his popularity? The awakening came later, much later,
after the war broke out, when my initial euphoria had
waned and my suspicions were gradually taking shape.
That was over twenty years ago, when we were living in
New York. If I'd told my wife the truth . . ."

Klinger fell silent although, or because, there was
something on the tip of his tongue.

"I'm now convinced that she had her suspicions, at
least. She never voiced them, although my dependence on
him was so blatant, it stared at me from every mirror.
What an absurd picture I must have presented to the
world around me! But, whether my wife knew or not, we
could never speak about it either then or later, not even
after my son's death. She let me have my way, acted as if
she knew nothing, turned a blind eye. She was indulgent
and understanding. A wonderful wife—too wonderful,
perhaps, because her indulgence proved to be uninten-
tional cruelty. The others who were in on the secret, if
they existed, did not make themselves known. They must
have been embarrassed by the situation, embarrassed by
my relationship with a servant and secretary, embarrassed
by the difference in our ages. None of them cared to

broach the subject of sex between two men, the divine conception of the unnatural. To whom? To me? I would have told them to go to hell, everyone knew that. In those who saw through me, the ecstasy in which I lived, my double life, aroused either revulsion or compassion. Compassion at best, but chiefly revulsion and utter disgust. Had someone else been involved, it would have aroused the same emotions in me. But I myself was smitten, and the smitten are always guiltless. I knew such men and had always shunned them. I detested their effeminate manners and affectations and persuaded myself that they were all like that. But Jakob was different. His masculinity was wholly natural—he was a man, no doubt about that. I was different too, but in what respect did I really differ from other men? Well, you observe yourself from within yourself; you don't see what others see. Sooner or later someone will publish a biography that illuminates the darker side of Julius Klinger the homo-sexual. I won't live to see it, but whatever they write about me, the truth lies in my books. In others it may lie elsewhere."

"I wasn't a voyeur," Erneste said. "There aren't any books about me."

"No," said Klinger.

He reached for his empty cup but didn't fill it.

"What was I supposed to think you were? I took you for a chance intruder, in fact I soon forgot all about you. Once I left the room, your face was expunged from my memory. Jakob never mentioned you while we were in

Giessbach. Doubtless he had his reasons for deluding me into believing myself the only one privileged to feast on his youth and his body, just as I had my reasons for believing him. I felt rejuvenated! And I was, too."

Klinger gave a sudden laugh.

"I was just as corrupt as Jakob. Each in our own way, we were convinced of the incontestable rightness of our conduct. That was the basis of our personal wellbeing, and what could be more important than our wellbeing, as long as we weren't hurting a third party? Nor were we, as long as he didn't find out. I didn't know of that third party's existence—I genuinely knew nothing about you, and it wouldn't have changed a thing if I had. That incident in the attic, which ought to have opened my eyes, was never mentioned. After all, what did it matter if another young man, a waiter who'd mistaken the door, had seen me indulging in my proclivity?

"We met in my own room after that. He never mentioned you until he discovered your uses as a weapon against me. The name of that weapon was youth and the target was my age—it couldn't fail. At some stage he started to use you against me, first you, then an assortment of young men he brought in off the street. That's why I probably know you better than you imagine. It's a long time ago, but I haven't forgotten it all, a few details have stuck in my mind. Jakob used his memories to torment me, and the memories best suited to hurting me were of you, his first love, the person who in his eyes surpassed me in every respect: youth, potency, lack of inhibition. You were the bullet that always hit the target. There was an even more lethal one, but of that I learned only later. It strayed into our convoluted relationship and killed someone else. Why did you come?"

"You used to pay him."

Klinger gave an almost imperceptible start.

"Five francs, don't you remember? Jakob got 5 francs a time. You used to put the money on the bed. You knew his terms—you knew he didn't love you, not for an instant. He did what he did of his own free will but not for nothing. Every time you needed him you had to give him 5 francs, I know that for a certainty because he kept a record of his takings—I saw the book myself. His attentions weren't a gift, they were services rendered in return for payment received. You paid him in advance, didn't you? You trusted him implicitly, and I'm sure he never bilked you. Jakob wasn't just perfect, he was unique. You paid cash and got Jakob. You got him only at a price."

While the words were escaping from Erneste's lips almost as fast as the thoughts running through his head, Klinger began to emerge from his state of petrifaction. For a moment Erneste thought he would break in, but he waited. Then he said slowly, "I told you, you had the advantage of me in every respect, but I still didn't realize that. I was convinced of my own importance."

"You had to go on paying him until his passage to America was signed and sealed," Erneste continued. "And even after that, perhaps?" Klinger said nothing. "Up to the time I caught you together in our room, you'd paid him a total of 45 Swiss francs for his services. I checked that carefully, and I still remember it because I haven't forgotten a thing, unfortunately. You knew what you were buying and he knew what he was being paid for. By the time I burst in on you, he'd already put himself at your disposal nine times."

"Perhaps."

"Jakob knew what he was worth. He knew his price. I felt I had a right to know the truth, so I went through his things and found his cashbook in the wardrobe we shared. I immediately came across your initials and the row of figures, all fives, nine of them: nine blow jobs at 5 francs apiece. But they were a good deal for you as well as him. You got Jakob on the cheap, really, a handsome youngster like him. And then you held out the prospect of America and freedom."

"Yes," said Klinger, "he couldn't be accused of lacking a head for business, but I'd have paid a great deal more to acquire him. He had only to ask and he'd have gotten it all, he knew that. I realized he didn't love me, but I needed him. Not his conversation, not his understanding, not even his affection. All I needed was that young man, his smell, his body, his absence of constraint—the fact that he did what I wanted when it suited him, that he was at my disposal, that he was willing: the sheer ownership of that body. I couldn't have cared less how that inestimable treasure came into my possession, I wanted to have it and keep it. I had to pay him for being the first to offer me a chance of what I'd craved for so long but had been too afraid to ask for. I wanted something"—Klinger hesitated—"I'd never had before. For years I'd waited, gnawed by a calamitous desire that sapped my strength and had to be assuaged. A frenzied god was crying out inside me for release. I was nearly fifty. I couldn't have gone on living like that any longer, I had no choice. I needed Jakob in order to survive—Jakob, my fire-bringing, life-giving Prometheus—before I myself became a Prometheus whose innards were daily devoured anew. For a while he enabled me to forget that my youth was over, that I'd missed out on nearly everything I'd longed for since my early days. That yearning, which had steadily intensified in recent years, became physically perceptible during those last few turbulent months in Europe. It was a nightly yearning that scorched and froze my body in turn. I couldn't and wouldn't die without doing what had obsessed me for as long as I could remember: I had to touch a man, and for that no price was too high. I appeased the god raging inside me with a vice I managed to conceal from others. Had Jakob demanded it of me, I would genuinely have prayed to him—kneeled down before him like a worshiper before an altar. I was demented and done for. Jakob fulfilled me entirely. All I could think of was: 'To America, quickly. To America, our Promised Land.' "

164

Erneste left the attic room soon after Klinger. He might have said he needed some fresh air because he genuinely did, he couldn't remember. Meantime, Jakob remained silent. He didn't attempt to find words to explain his behavior, which seemed self-explanatory in any case. Instead of rendering the situation slightly less irredeemable, he left it in the air by saying nothing. He didn't apologize or attempt to justify himself. At length he got to his feet, frozen-faced and seemingly at a loss, with reddish patches visible on his knees. And because Erneste couldn't endure his own distress or the sight of Jakob's reddened knees and helpless expression, he turned tail. He turned on his heel and went out because nothing could prevent him from taking flight, which was possibly the worst thing he'd ever done. Instead of forgiving Jakob, he left him on his own. He felt he was suffocating, in need of air.

In search of some task that might have taken his mind off things, he wandered through the hotel but failed to find anyone who needed his services. The kitchen and terrace were deserted, the bar was closed, and there was no one in the lobby but the receptionist. He left the building by a side entrance, plunged straight out into the sunlight and started walking. It was just after two. In the last few minutes his life had been turned inside out like a glove. The pain was relentless; it became more intense with every breath, every step, every memory. He hadn't been mistaken: Jakob hadn't been the same for a long time. He was a different person since returning from Germany in the spring. Jakob didn't need him anymore. He'd been going his own way ever since then.

Erneste had left the hotel in his waiter's outfit although staff were requested always to wear plain clothes off the premises, but he took care not to run into anyone, not wanting to be seen and compelled to talk. Without debating which way to go, he headed down through the woods to the lake, stumbling occasionally because he was walking too fast. He passed the spot where they had kissed for the first time and came to a halt in the middle of the path, abruptly convulsed with despair. Then he continued on his way to the lakeshore, where he spent a long time gazing at the water. When a steamer laden with passengers approached he turned back.

Jakob was gone by the time he returned to their room. It was now three o'clock. Too late, nothing to be done, it was over. He suddenly felt so dizzy from the heat and his exertions, he had to lie down. He pulled off his dusty black shoes. The thing he'd sometimes dreamed of had happened. It wasn't a nightmare, it had happened precisely where he was at this moment. He had only to look around to confirm that.

———·•·———

For two days they didn't exchange a word. They couldn't always avoid each other, but their different working hours were a boon when it came to taking evasive action. Erneste held his breath and pretended to be asleep when Jakob entered their room in the small hours, and he hardly dared swallow when Jakob lay down beside him. They didn't even exchange a glance for two whole days, though they couldn't help meeting in their room in the afternoons.

Erneste felt as if he was walking through a wall, and it cost him an effort to make out the objects in the room. Incapable of lucid thought, he was equally incapable of speaking out. Although he had a pretty clear idea of how this endless torment could be ended, he didn't end it. They lay there mutely side by side.

Erneste felt sure that Jakob was continuing to see Klinger, but the indirect confirmation of his suspicions exceeded all his worst fears. On the third day Jakob informed him that he'd spoken to Herr Direktor Wagner and handed in his notice. Those were the first words that had passed between them after two days of silence. They were said by the by, so to speak, just as Erneste was about to leave the room. He let go of the door handle. No words could have hit him harder.

Jakob had sat up in bed. The baneful announcement was brief and to the point: "I spoke to the manager today. I've quit."

"What do you mean?"

"I'm leaving. I'm off to America in a few weeks' time."

"America? Why?"

"Klinger needs a manservant. I'm going with him."

"I see. You'll make a good manservant."

"I think so too. I've got to get away from here."

"Away from me."

"Away from here. If there's a war, and there will be, I'd have to go back to Cologne. Everyone says so—Klinger says so. And I don't want to go back."

"Klinger says so, and you're going with him. He's rescuing you."

Jakob nodded. "Yes, he's helping me."

Outwardly composed but without grasping the significance of the words, Erneste said, "And I'll stay on here and wait for the war to end. Everything will sort itself out in due course."

He had been prepared for anything, but not for the fact that Jakob's future had long been settled behind his back without a moment's thought being given to the possibility that this might determine his future too.

Nothing could prevent Jakob from leaving him for good. Klinger had already made arrangements to do as Jakob wished. Jakob had opted for Klinger because he knew that Klinger would opt for him. Klinger could be helpful to Jakob, that was undeniable. Jakob would accompany him and his family to America as a lover in the guise of a manservant. When Erneste envisaged the full extent of this upheaval, he thought he was losing his mind. But the condition didn't last. He didn't lose his mind. He went on working as if nothing had happened.

"When passion becomes a slaveholder," said Klinger, "it becomes dangerous. Jakob didn't love me, whereas all I wanted was to possess him to the exclusion of everything and everyone else. Knowing this, he exploited it and despised me for it. His own role he ignored—he didn't think it contemptible at all. Later on, not long after the war, I wrote a novella, *The Wound*, which presented a veiled account of our liaison. It was a thorough failure because my treatment of what I ought to have written about was deficient in the extreme. I made no attempt to write the truth, I lacked the courage, so everything remained superficial. I described the disastrous love of an older man for a younger woman who drives him insane, not the love of one man for another man who reduces him to a cipher and almost obliterates him. I never even tried to be truthful in *The Wound*; I simply skirted around the truth regardless of any loss of veracity. I lacked courage, so I became a liar. All I produced, alas, was a repetition of something far from unique in literature, yet my little novella was regarded as verging on the scandalous, so it attracted a lot of publicity. What an uproar it would have caused had I written even a fraction of what I *could* have written! But it was even filmed—perhaps you've heard of the picture. It was just another step down the road to obfuscation. My due reward for abusing the truth was a second-rate cast, a mediocre director and an opportunistic scriptwriter. My novella ends with a murder. The film begins with a murder and is one long justification of that murder. The murderer's guilt is relativized and, thus, excused.

My story, the true story, ended quite differently. That's the story I should have written, but I couldn't—I never even tried because the time isn't ripe for such stories. Mark my words, though, in twenty or thirty years' time it may be possible to write a story like that. If I'd kept a diary, which I never have, alas, the story of my dependence on Jakob would be documented in every detail and available for everyone to read: an account of what a man can suffer and what can be done to him. Sadly, it was not to be. You, Monsieur Erneste, are the only person I've ever told. I didn't devote a single word to Jakob in my memoirs. They break off when I emigrate to America, and there won't be a sequel. It would be nice if I could say I shall die in peace, at one with myself and the story of my life, but that isn't so. And I fear my story doesn't interest you particularly. On the other hand, I can only tell it to someone who knows it but is utterly indifferent to it. Because, of course, I mean absolutely nothing to you."

"As little as you did when you took Jakob away from me, or when I saw things in that light. Of course, he was simply doing what he wanted."

The tea had gone cold. A fly was squatting on Erneste's saucer. He stared at the slices of cake on the plate. Frau Moser hadn't reappeared. Klinger's house was pervaded by an almost soothing hush.

"And now, tell me why you came. What do you want?"

"Jakob has written to me. I've received two letters from him."

"You're in contact with him?"

"In a manner of speaking."

"You've been in contact with him all this time?"

"Not at all. I hadn't heard from him for thirty years. I didn't even know if he was still living in America—if he was still alive, even."

"So he's alive."

"Yes."

"What does he want?"

"He asked me to get in touch with you."

"Why?"

Erneste took Jakob's letters from his breast pocket and put them down beside the tray. Klinger glanced at them. He evidently recognized Jakob's handwriting, but ingrained reserve forbade him to reach for them at once.

"What's it about?"

"Money."

Erneste stared at the letters intently, almost as if they might dissolve into thin air.

"I'm here as his go-between," he said. "That's the role he assigned me. He wants you to help him financially. That's my job."

"Is he sick?"

"No. At least, I don't think so."

Erneste handed Klinger the letters. He didn't take his eyes off him during the minutes that followed. Klinger put his glasses on. His expression underwent a gradual change. "Nobel Prize . . . plenty of cash . . . FBI . . . Weston . . ." He rose to his feet, occasionally muttering the words aloud as he read them. Then, abruptly, he froze and looked down at Erneste.

"He must be insane, absolutely insane, to think he can melt my heart with these fairy tales. Weston, Burlington and the rest of those witch hunters—they drowned in their own mire long ago. Times have changed, nobody's after me anymore. I'm a man of repute in the States as well."

Erneste shrugged. "You must help him all the same."

"How old and ugly he must have become, and how low he's sunk, to have to resort to such tricks. You can't be frightened of people who've lost all their clout. The men he talks about, the ones he claims are after him, have long been completely devoid of influence. Their boss died ten years ago. How uninformed does he think I am?"

"You won't help him?"

Klinger sat down again. He replaced the letters on the table and removed his glasses.

"I couldn't even if I wanted to. He should know that."

"Why not?"

Overcome by a fit of uncontrollable agitation whose sudden violence even he found surprising, Erneste jumped to his feet and shouted the words again and again. His question remained unanswered. Klinger, who was unprepared to reply, called Frau Moser. He slumped a little in his chair and shook his head, but that was no answer. Moments later Frau Moser entered the room, in which the fading daylight only dimly disclosed the two men's drained and exhausted faces. She looked from one to the other, then signed to Erneste to accompany her. He didn't demur. He picked up the letters, pocketed them, and turned to go. Without bidding Klinger goodbye, he silently left the room in which his cries still seemed to linger in the air. By the harsh glare of a flash of lightning, real or imaginary, the scene underwent a transformation, and he left the room feeling just as he had when leaving that other room in Giessbach thirty years before. Where Jakob had been kneeling, Klinger now sat, and where Erneste stood, Erneste stood again, beyond anyone's power to help. He felt the door handle just as he had felt it then, although this time he didn't touch it because the door by which he left the room was open. He went out into the hallway. Frau Moser walked ahead of him to the front door, where she took leave of him with a nod. The attic room was now deserted. And so, from one moment to the next, he returned from the past to the present. He walked back down the hill, made his way through the village to the station, sat down on a bench on the platform, and waited for the next train. He looked at his watch: another seventeen minutes.

Twelve minutes later he got up and left the station. He walked through the village again and headed back to Klinger's house, striding along quickly and purposefully now that he knew the way and had no need to ask for directions. When he came to Klinger's gate he rang the bell again and again, but he guessed, even as he pressed the button for the first time, that no one would answer. He was unwanted now. To that extent he now resembled

Jakob and had been put on a par with him. That lent him a certain strength. Now that they knew who he was and what he wanted, they were deaf to his plea.

―――――――

Erneste got up early the day after his visit to Klinger. He had a bath and shaved, and while shaving he inspected his face closely in the mirror. He managed to examine it with the eye of a stranger. Although traces of his beating were still visible, they were now so faint, he had no need to fear that they would arouse unwelcome suspicions. He could go back to work with an easy mind.

An hour later—he walked there as usual—he entered the Restaurant am Berg by the tradesmen's entrance and was surprised to find that his reappearance was greeted with pleasure, not only by the manager but also by his fellow waiters—even by the chefs and kitchen hands. Although none of them slapped him on the back, still less inquired the reason for his absence, he could tell from their friendly faces that they had missed him a little and might even have been worried about him. Erneste resumed work as if he had never been away. He supervised the tables in the Blue Room, which were just being set, checked the position of the napkins and the arrangement of the cutlery and glasses. For the first few hours, during which he occasionally undertook minor adjustments with an economical touch, he felt thoroughly at ease in his accustomed environment. He wasn't a guest or visitor here; he was at home, having been given to understand that he was needed. He even exerted himself rather more than usual for the next few days, blind to everything that happened outside his work.

He had his reasons, because he was naturally aware that he had achieved nothing. He tried to act as if all was well, but not even the hardest work could blind him to the reality of his utter failure. His attempt to gain a hearing had misfired. He had come away empty-handed, and that was a shattering blow. It wasn't Jakob who had failed, nor was it Klinger, who had refused to help; it was himself, Erneste, who had tried to help in vain. Klinger had used him to unburden himself by airing a secret he might well have taken to the grave but for Erneste's appearance on the scene. Erneste hadn't been sent for; he had come of his own volition. Perhaps his visit had injected some welcome but fundamentally unimportant variety into Klinger's life. Just a brushstroke, a dab of paint on the fading palette of his existence.

Erneste was troubled by the thought that his mission had achieved precisely nothing, so he tried to take his mind off this by concentrating on his work. He succeeded in banishing Jakob from his mind for as long as customers and colleagues claimed his attention, and whenever the thought of Jakob did cross his mind he shooed it away like a troublesome fly and readdressed himself to his various duties. He was assisted in this by two social functions, a big dinner on Friday night and a first-night party on the Saturday. Among those he waited on were a world-famous

Swedish tenor and an English conductor whose glances in his direction were so unambiguous that he felt startled rather than flattered. His mementos of the latter occasion were the Swedish tenor's autograph and the conductor's languishing gaze. A lot of eating and drinking was done both nights, so he had his hands full. The tenor and the Romanian prima donna attracted great attention when they left, whereas the conductor's departure passed almost unnoticed. He gave Erneste a last, silent look as he helped him on with his coat and slipped a visiting card into his pocket. There was a phone number scribbled on the back.

———·•·———

By Sunday morning, if not before, Erneste could shelve the thought of Jakob no longer. Wide awake at seven o'clock, only four hours after going to bed, he lay staring at his open wardrobe. He had a headache—everything gave him a headache these days. Jakob was waiting impatiently. He was waiting in the wardrobe, waiting among his clothes and the objects lying around. He was waiting here, waiting in New York, waiting for an answer, for a letter, money, help, but he'd even been denied a refusal. The only person who could answer him was too cowardly to do so. Writing to Jakob was out of the question, for Jakob was uninterested in the truth. On the other hand, Erneste didn't want to lie to him, so he wouldn't write, not yet. He couldn't act unaided. To act he needed Klinger's help, but Klinger had refused it and would continue to do so unless he did something, so something had to be done. There was only one way out of this apparent impasse: he must bring pressure to bear on Klinger. There was only one thing to do and he would do it.

At eight he got up and had some coffee. Two cups, three, four. He didn't touch the bread, butter and jelly he'd set out on the kitchen table as if this were an ordinary Sunday. Taking a sheet of paper, he wrote Klinger's phone number at the top and beneath it his ultimatum. He went to the window and looked down at the street, then across at the house opposite, the one in which his unknown neighbor's shadow bobbed up and down in the small hours. The light was still on, so she'd probably dozed off after a sleepless night. The morning was cold. He put on a sweater and his overcoat, then left the apartment, buttoning up his coat against the chilly wind. The street was deserted. He set off for the phone booth, walking as fast as if he were in a hurry, which he wasn't.

The phone booth stank of urine and one of the panes was smeared with filth. A week ago the phone book had been intact. Since then, someone had wantonly torn some of its pages out of the cover. A few of them lay crumpled on the floor amid banana skins and other trash, but the phone itself was working.

Erneste unfolded the sheet of paper, smoothed it out on the shelf, and dialed Klinger's number. The receiver was heavy, the earpiece cold. He waited for Frau Moser to answer. She didn't sound surprised to hear his voice, just asked what he wanted. "I must speak to Herr Klinger," he said. "It's very urgent." Frau Moser said, "I believe you, but you know he doesn't take calls in the morning. Never, not from anyone. Call back this afternoon. He's working."

"I have to speak to him *now*. I can't wait any longer."

"I'm not allowed to disturb him in the morning."

"I know that, but I've *got* to speak to him! What I have to say to him is more important than his work. He can go back to work as soon as I've said it."

"I'll see what I can do, but don't get your hopes up." She put the receiver down and Erneste waited. While he was waiting and wondering if she really had gone to confer with Klinger or was simply holding her hand over the receiver, he turned and looked down the street. Nothing was stirring. The absence of movement matched his own situation.

Since Klinger had refused to come to the phone right away and would probably refuse to speak with him on any subsequent occasion, Erneste asked Frau Moser to give him the following message: Unless he announced his readiness to make the requisite arrangements to help Jakob, he, Erneste, would approach some of the less reputable newspapers and acquaint them with certain aspects of Klinger's private life. They would undoubtedly be interested in such details, because nothing was too smutty for them not to exploit it to the full. Erneste's agitation was such that he raised his voice, but his fears proved groundless: he didn't lose his composure or become incoherent—he didn't even have to consult his notes. His ultimatum came over loud and clear. The tabloids, he went on, made a living out of exposing the intimate secrets of well-known personalities. They certainly wouldn't pass up an opportunity to wash Klinger's dirty linen in public. They were notorious for their readiness to injure the reputations of prominent citizens or ruin them altogether, and Klinger must surely be aware that any damage to his own reputation would damage the reputation of those associated with him, notably politicians like the cantonal president, who had recently conferred honorary citizenship on him. Erneste would not only sell the gutter press such details as he knew, he could assure Klinger of that; if necessary, he would invent a few more. He had nothing to lose, whereas Klinger stood to lose a great deal. His good name and reputation were at stake. Erneste would use the money he made from his revelations to help Jakob to the best of his ability, but none of this would be necessary if Klinger agreed to help—help Jakob, of course, not himself. His sole concern was Jakob, who was in a desperate predicament.

"But that's blackmail," Frau Moser said when Erneste fell silent at last. "Yes," he said, "you're absolutely right. It's the first time I've done such a thing, and I'm sure it'll be the last, but in this particular case I've no choice."

Before hanging up he asked Frau Moser to make a note of his address. "I shall expect to hear from Herr Klinger."

———•———

Erneste went home and spent the rest of the morning in his bedroom, lying fully dressed on the bed and staring at the ceiling. He was hungry but ate nothing. Later he turned on the radio beside his bed. The reception on the other stations was poor, so he listened as usual to Radio Beromünster: church service, the news, an orchestral concert. No *Postillon de Longjumeau* on this last Sunday in October, much as he would have liked to hear it. The voice of the woman announcing the titles of the pieces was familiar to him, so he found it easy to daydream idly to the accompaniment of Puccini's *Crisantemi.*

At lunchtime he opened a can of ravioli, heated the can in a saucepan of water, and ate half of it with two glasses of white wine and water. The rest he threw away. He didn't shave, there was time for that. He was going to make himself some more coffee but drank another glass of wine instead, undiluted this time. No coffee, he'd run out of milk. If he'd had to, he would have waited forty-eight hours for Klinger's reply without moving. But it wasn't necessary.

Shortly after seven—he still hadn't shaved—a taxi pulled up outside. The bell on the black box above his front door rang. He wasn't expecting anyone. He pressed the buzzer, opened the door and put his head out, listening. He heard the shuffling footsteps of someone toiling up the stairs to the second floor. He withdrew his head, leaving the door ajar, and hurried to the bathroom, where he glanced in the mirror and ran a comb through his hair.

He started to tremble when he peeked through the spy hole, even though he'd guessed it was Klinger—even though that was the obvious conclusion. He stepped aside just as Klinger pushed the door open.

The old man had clearly found the stairs an effort. He was breathing heavily and looked exhausted. His ocher-colored camel-hair coat, hat, scarf, gloves, gleaming oxfords—all were of the finest quality. Erneste felt positively squalid in comparison. He hadn't aired his apartment for days or received any visitors since Julie. He was unprepared, but this didn't seem to bother Klinger. As if it were unnecessary to take any notice of him, he simply said, "I need to sit down."

"Please come in," said Erneste.

He had been expecting either a bearer check or a refusal, not a visit from the man himself. Klinger had taken the trouble to come in person, so the matter must be urgent. His audacity was paying off.

He apologized for his get-up—"It's Sunday"—and for the mess prevailing in his apartment, but Klinger was interested neither in his appearance nor in the state of his apartment. He took off his hat. Erneste hung it on a hook in the hallway, then conducted him into the living room, shutting the bedroom door on the way. The bed was unmade and there were dirty clothes lying on the floor, but Klinger didn't seem to notice. He sat down in one of the two armchairs and said, "Please bring me a glass of water."

Erneste went to the kitchen. He turned on the faucet and let the water run for a few moments. Then he remembered that there was an unopened bottle of mineral water in the fridge. Before taking it out he reached for the white wine and swigged some straight from the bottle, having first satisfied himself that Klinger couldn't see him from the armchair. He was feeling rather dizzy. He could hardly offer Klinger wine from an open bottle, so what else? A brandy, maybe? He put the mineral water and two glasses on a tray. Klinger had come on his own. Had he called the police? Had he laid a charge of blackmail against this lowly waiter who had overstepped the mark? Erneste was a foreigner. Would they deport him? He glanced out the window. The street was deserted except for a man outside the house next door, thumbing the doorbell and looking up at the windows with an irresolute air. His neighbor's light was on, but there was no sign of the woman herself. Klinger evidently wasn't in the habit of getting other people to do his business for him. He knew what he wanted—he still had time to go to the police. His options were open.

There he sat in Erneste's living room, visible in semiprofile and looking vaguely out of place in his overcoat, as if this were only a flying visit. Erneste came in bearing the tray with the water and the glasses. Putting it down on his oval coffee table, which had a colored mosaic top, he unscrewed the bottle cap and filled the glasses, first Klinger's, then his own. He remained standing.

Klinger looked up. "Always the perfect waiter," he said, "even in his own home." Erneste couldn't tell whether he was commending him or simply being sarcastic. Klinger raised his right hand a trifle and let it fall. He looked tired.

He waited until Erneste had sat down. Then he slowly unbuttoned his overcoat and produced an envelope from the breast pocket. He put the letter on the table. Erneste saw that it bore a United States stamp and was addressed in typescript. Picking it up again, Klinger turned it over in his hands before tapping the tabletop with the edge of the envelope.

"From Jakob?" Erneste asked softly.

"Yes and no. It was sent me care of my New York publishers. I received it four days after your visit. It contains some news. Bad news. I shouldn't have kept it from you, but I waited. It's over. This letter renders your attempt to blackmail me superfluous."

"Why? Has Jakob written to you direct?"

"No, this letter isn't from Jakob." Klinger turned it over. "It's from a man named Gingold." He paused. "Neither of us could have known this when you visited me, but Jakob was already dead." A huge hand gripped Erneste by the throat and squeezed. He couldn't speak, couldn't move, couldn't stand up or breathe.

Klinger replaced the envelope on the table face up and tapped it with his forefinger. "This contains a death notice. A death notice and a letter from Mr Gingold." He took out a sheet of paper and a pale-gray card with a black border. The latter was adorned with a palm leaf, a cross, and the words *The Lord is my shepherd. Jack Meier 1914–1966.*

"According to Mr Gingold—a close friend of Jakob's, one presumes—he died of a cerebral tumor. It was diagnosed far too late. He consulted a doctor three months ago, because he was suffering from unbearable headaches, but by that time his condition was hopeless, the tumor was too far advanced. There was nothing to be done. They couldn't operate because of the tumor's location and size—it would have been extremely risky under any circumstances. The tumor continued to grow unchecked at an incredible rate—'incredible', that's the word Mr Gingold uses. It also gave rise to the mental confusion that prompted him to write you those letters. A cerebral tumor can cause all kinds of manic delusions. His erroneous belief that he was being tailed by the FBI men who once shadowed me, compelling me to leave the States and return to Europe, was simply a delusion occasioned by the tumor. He thought he needed help, but he was financially secure and well provided for. You weren't to know that, neither was I, but it wouldn't have surprised either of us to hear he was down on his luck, would it? This American friend of Jakob's didn't learn of his letters to you until he was dead. Jakob was already in another world, his world of illusion, when he wrote them. By then he was beyond help—in fact he was probably dead by the time you heard from him the second time." Klinger unfolded the letter. "Those headaches of his were agonizing, Mr Gingold writes. The pain didn't ease until they started dosing him heavily with morphine. He didn't suffer for much longer after that, it seems, because he was granted a quick and merciful death. He didn't die alone—he had good doctors and kindly nurses. Two days before his death he went blind and lost consciousness. He was past recognizing anyone."

Klinger pushed the death notice across to Erneste, who stared at it. "He was only fifty-two."

Erneste's one thought was: "I heard him correctly, I'll never see Jakob again." He repeated the words to himself: "I heard him correctly, I'll never see Jakob again." He *had* heard him correctly, he *would* never see Jakob again—never be able to forgive him. The walls of the room in which they were sitting collapsed, slowly and silently, like a house of cards. Erneste and his agony of mind could now be viewed from every angle. He didn't care, though, not now he possessed the key to the truth: Jakob was dead and needed no help.

"Who is this Gingold?"

Klinger shrugged. Neither of them spoke. At length, Klinger picked up his glass and drained it. Later he poured himself another glass, but Erneste barely noticed. He had been wrested from a years-long sleep and was now being relegated to it once more. Was that all that remained of him, three sentences: "I won't see Jakob again. Did I hear him correctly? Yes, I did."

"So your attempt to blackmail me has become irrelevant. Let's forget it." Abruptly, Klinger went on: "His death was a sad but well-merited punishment for his depravity." Erneste stared at him uncomprehendingly. Klinger made no move to rise. "You really mean that?" Erneste asked. But Klinger didn't answer; he was as opaque as the objects around him. "Do you have any photos of him?" he asked.

Erneste remained silent. Yes, he had some photos. They were somewhere down in the cellar, but he wouldn't go looking for them.

12

A few days after the United States declared war on December 7, 1941, Julius Klinger and his wife went to the opera, but they returned home earlier than intended because Marianne was feeling unwell that night. Klinger disliked the performance so much, he was quite happy to leave the theater after the first act.

It was snowing when they came out onto the street. They hadn't owned a car since moving to Manhattan, so they went home by cab. Jakob, who had been informed of their return by the porter, was waiting for them at the door of their apartment.

Frau Moser had gone out with a woman friend that night and Josefa was sitting in the library, playing solitaire. Jakob reported that Maximilian had retired to his room to study early that evening and hadn't shown his face since. Klinger asked what sort of mood Maxi was in, but Jakob shrugged and said he didn't know. When Klinger tried to touch him, Jakob evaded his hand and it closed on thin air—for the very last time, not that he would ever have dreamed it at that moment. Klinger stared after him. His craving for

Jakob's body was as inordinate and insatiable as ever, a source of unhappiness yet not entirely unsatisfying. He was now fifty-three, Jakob twenty-five.

The hush prevailing in the apartment, the snow falling outside, the subdued lighting—all these accorded with Klinger's present frame of mind. A better future seemed to beckon. America's entry into the war and its readiness to overthrow Hitler at any price, even the loss of American lives in battle, was heartening and liberating. He would have liked to discuss the future with someone, but he knew how reluctant Josefa was to have her games of solitaire interrupted and how little interest Maximilian, now a law student, took in his father's concerns. Besides, the boy was unapproachable these days. Taciturn and distant, he had become more and more remote from the family since their arrival in America.

Klinger glanced at his watch: half-past ten. He looked out the window—it was snowing even harder—and resumed his aimless tour of the apartment. It was time to bring the day to an end, but the futility with which the seconds were ticking away deterred him. He was in no hurry. Did this soothing silence conceal some disruptive element? If so, he couldn't place it. In an hour or so he would ask Jakob to bring him a cup of tea in bed. What would or would not happen then, time would tell.

Marianne Klinger had retired to bed and would not emerge from her room until morning. Her room was a desert island. No palm trees grew there, just memories of days gone by—a vast and luxuriant store of memories kept alive by the innumerable souvenirs with which she surrounded herself, having long led a life of her own. It was twenty to eleven and still snowing when Klinger turned out the light in his study, which adjoined his bedroom, which in turn adjoined Jakob's. All three rooms had communicating doors, so Jakob was always available if he needed him. He left his study, which contained his desk and Jakob's smaller, uncluttered desk with its big American typewriter. Klinger's Adler had been left behind in Germany.

While his daughter was playing solitaire and Jakob busying himself with something in the kitchen, Klinger ambled through the spacious apartment, which was on the ninth floor of an eighteen story building. The third time he passed Maximilian's room he felt tempted to knock on his door. It was so quiet in there, the boy had probably fallen asleep over his law books. If he really was asleep, Klinger reflected, he wouldn't hear the door open. But he abandoned the idea. Not wanting to disturb his son, he strolled on from room to room. The lighting was the way he liked it: subdued, never bright, and shed by at least one standard or table lamp in every room. His daughter glanced up from her solitaire as he passed the library again. She gave him a cursory nod, smiled, and quickly put down two cards. She looked so grown-up, so old, so remote. Didn't she have a girlfriend, a boyfriend? Eleven o'clock now. He was in the drawing room. He opened the door of the grandfather clock that had accompanied him for years and wound it up as he did every night. He sat down, waiting, listening. Yes, all was quiet. Too quiet? Exactly how many paces away were his son, his daughter, his wife, Jakob? He would never know, nor did it seem important at that moment.

The tranquil silence was abruptly punctured by the sound of a door crashing back against a wall. Then he heard hurried footsteps making for the drawing room— making for him, beyond a doubt, and since he recognized those footsteps he wasn't surprised when Jakob appeared in the doorway.

Jakob paused on the threshold, his expression as unequivocal as the sound of his uncharacteristically hurried footsteps had been alarming: something had happened that shouldn't have happened. "Maxi," he said softly, as if the others mustn't hear what he had to say. "Maxi . . ." He said it one more time, then his voice failed him, and Klinger, who couldn't know what had happened, sensed that this was no time for questions, so he didn't ask any. He jumped up and followed Jakob along the passage. Jakob hurried on ahead, and Klinger realized that he was on the verge of losing his composure without knowing why. He would know why very soon, but he wouldn't lose his composure after all.

He followed Jakob into Maxi's room. The nameless fear that had gripped him proved to be justified. His son lay stretched out on the bed only a few feet away, his face a yellowish, waxen shade. That wasn't a normal complexion, it was the color of death. What business had he in Maximilian's room if Maximilian couldn't call him? The light was on. Turned on by whom? Maxi was wearing a dark suit Klinger had never seen before, a new one, perhaps, with his bare feet protruding from the trousers. No socks or shoes. He was wearing a jacket and trousers, a white shirt, a dark-blue tie, a gold stickpin with a green stone. Jacket and trousers, shirt, tie, stickpin.

Jacket and trousers, shirt, tie, stickpin. Dark-blue and gold, and peeking out of the trouser legs his bare feet, almost a boy's feet, yellowish like his face and even more naked in appearance. He looked as if he had climbed out of his body after death, as if he had bent down and rearranged his limbs—possibly even raised the drooping corners of his mouth to make death look less terrible. He hadn't succeeded, though, because he himself was death, he himself looked terrible irrespective of the expression on his face. He had forgotten to do up the zipper on his trousers and was wearing no under-pants. Abashed and dismayed, Klinger averted his gaze. His dead son was wearing no underpants. Why not, if he hadn't left anything else to chance? Klinger felt he had glimpsed the flesh of Maxi's penis. It might have been his imagination, a deceptive trick of the light, but he didn't want to see it, nor did he have to see it for long, because Jakob proceeded to do what he, the boy's father, should have done. The action that should have come quite naturally to Maxi's father came quite naturally to his manservant and lover. It was Jakob, not he, who bent over Maxi. Carefully, as if afraid of hurting the dead youth, the hand Klinger had so often held in his pulled up the zipper and concealed his son's dead flesh from his gaze, the piece of flesh whose function it was to give pleasure and create life. Klinger was overcome by a nausea such as he had never experienced before and would never experience again, a feeling that he, who believed himself capable of describing anything and everything, although he had not yet done so, would never be able to describe. He had no power over the destinies of the living. If they died they stayed dead, and there was nothing—no eraser or stroke of the pen—that could undo the death of a real person. A simple truth: his son was dead, but he hadn't died a natural death. The objects that had been nearest him at the last—the bottle of gin, the sleeping tablets—were eloquent enough. He had communed with those objects and they had communed with him, but now that he had fallen silent they were communing with themselves alone. Curiously enough, although Julius Klinger was forever finding new words for the unendurable, the proper emotions eluded him. He couldn't understand what had happened.

It looked as if Maximilian had tried to fold his hands in death. At the same time, however, it looked as if someone else had tried to wrench his folded hands apart, and the latter attempt had been more successful than the former, so only his fingertips were touching.

What a sight: his own son, dead in New York. Twenty-two years old. Three years younger than Jakob, thirty-one years younger than himself. What was the significance of the bare feet? Why wasn't he wearing any socks? Why the dark suit, the clean shirt, the tie, but no shoes? What would that have signified in a book, in one of his own novels? It wasn't hard to guess what had happened or imagine what lay in store for himself and his family. Klinger could see it all quite clearly. It was now up to him to knock on his wife's bedroom door, to wake her up, to forewarn her of "something terrible" and conduct her to her dead son's room, her beloved and only son's room. He would of course do this in the end. For the moment, though, he stood motionless some three feet from the end of the bed, staring at his son's bare feet. And while he was wondering why Jakob was bending over Maximilian and putting his left hand behind the boy's head and raising it as if he meant to kiss him, he saw out of the corner of his eye that there was an envelope tucked between the pages of the law book lying on the bedside table. Without thinking, he plucked it out and slipped it into his pocket. Jakob noticed nothing. Later he found that the envelope had not been addressed, but the deceased was his son, so this last letter belonged to him.

And so, while he was wondering what Jakob was doing and why, Klinger, who had still not touched his own, only son, appropriated the envelope because he suspected that its contents presented a threat to himself and his family's peace of mind. Although only a suspicion, it was no less compelling than a certainty. Perhaps the letter said something that presented far more of a threat to him than Maximilian's death—an abominable thought, he reflected, thinking of himself. He was going through a tunnel and could see no light at the end, but he knew that he would get there someday. Not now, not tomorrow, but someday. All who traversed a tunnel reached the light in the end. The light or freedom.

Watching his lover and his son, Klinger saw Jakob close Maxi's eyes with his thumb and middle finger. He was watching a scene in which he had no allotted role. Only now did he grasp what had happened—what had happened a long time ago—and he was overcome by an incongruous emotion: jealousy.

He had never noticed anything. *He* had created this situation, not Jakob, not his son. What can a dead man do? Call something to us? Send us away? Was this the cathartic effect of dramatic intensity? Instead of summoning his wife he remained silent; instead of telling Jakob not to touch his son he said nothing. He was observing the scene of a lost battle; that was all he could do. He was condemned to be a war reporter, a painter of battle scenes. He did what a storyteller does: he looked around, noted details and instinctively memorized them. They would come in useful someday, but only when he could rearrange the decor. The bed on the left, the wardrobe on the right—and Jakob banished from the room.

The overhead light illuminated the scene with a merciless clarity appropriate to the dead youth and the objects that had facilitated his death. On the bedside table reposed an empty bottle of mineral water and a large tumbler, on the floor lay an overturned bottle of gin. The liquid spilled on the carpet had been absorbed, as witness the dark, damp patch and the faint scent of juniper that lingered in the air. Some sleeping tablets had fallen to the floor and dissolved in the moisture, forming fluffy white dots on the rug beside Maximilian's bed. They were the redundant tablets that had escaped from his fingers. No one would ever know what his last thoughts had been. All else was scrupulously neat and tidy.

"A doctor," Klinger whispered. "It's too late," Jakob said quietly. "Too late, he's dead."

"But why?" said Klinger. Jakob stared at him in bewilderment. "Why?"

Although Klinger had had a vague feeling that someone, somewhere in the background, was waiting for a sign from him, he'd ignored it because all his attention was focused on what was *not* moving. But now, when he heard a rustle and seemed to sense a draft on the back of his neck, he realized that it was his daughter who had been standing behind him, possibly for several seconds. She had continued to sit over her cards, listening, until she couldn't stand it anymore. Unwilling to wait until she was called and incapable of concentrating on her solitary game any longer, she had listened intently to the strange sounds coming from her brother's room. Now she had materialized behind her father and was shouting so loudly—shouting Maximilian's name in such a loud, anguished voice—that Klinger involuntarily turned and did something he had never done before: he hit her. He gave her such a slap that she reeled back into the doorway. He promptly regretted it, though he felt relieved and didn't apologize, composure being at odds with the situation. Needless to say, Josefa's cries alerted her mother.

Five people had crowded into Maximilian's room by the time Frau Moser entered it fifteen minutes later. The boy's body was obscured by the others, so she couldn't see it at first and took a few moments to fathom the situation. All she gathered, from the silence that lay heavy on all present, was that something momentous had occurred.

<hr />

While the sky outside grew steadily darker, Klinger described in a flat, unemotional voice how he had been granted the dubious pleasure of learning "the whole truth" that same night. The living-room light wasn't on, so he was visible only in silhouette, but Erneste didn't get up and turn on the ceiling light, which had a yellowish mock alabaster bowl. He needed the darkness. He didn't want to see Klinger, but he wanted to hear what had happened. His mouth was parched and he was trembling, his back and thighs bathed in sweat. He felt he hadn't washed for days. The air smelled of flowers although he never kept flowers in his apartment, and it wasn't Klinger that smelled of them.

When the doctor, a Viennese refugee, had filled out the death certificate and given Marianne Klinger a sedative before leaving, Klinger abandoned the others and shut himself up in his study. There, in the room where he wrote his books and dictated his letters and appeals, he sat down at his desk and tore open the envelope containing his son's bequest to him, a letter dashed off in a frenzy. He read and reread it, scanning the hurried lines again and again.

"I didn't read the letter once or twice that night, but twenty or thirty times. I skimmed it at first, then let every word eat its way into me, consume me, over and over again. I've no idea what the others thought— whether they wondered why I wasn't with them and why I didn't offer them any consolation or support. They may have believed I wanted to spare them the sight of my grief, when my only wish was not to confront them with the truth. I simply suppressed it because, if it had become known, my reputation would have suffered. No, I never had any intention of revealing the truth about me and my son, either then or later."

"So why now?"

"Because you called me. Because Jakob is also dead now. I'd almost forgotten him. Perhaps, too, because death is now closer to me than anything else. There's no real explanation."

"*I'm* still alive."

"And you can bear to hear the truth. You are, as I already said, a perfect waiter."

"Yes, that's been my lifelong ambition. I wanted Jakob to be one too. He didn't quite manage it, unfortunately."

"Who knows?"

Erneste started to get up. He gripped the arms of his chair with both hands but sensed the other man's eyes upon him and sat back again. "No, hear me out," Klinger said. It was impossible to evade or interrupt him.

"My son's farewell letter was brutally brief. It dealt with his existence ever since that day in Giessbach when Jakob came into our lives—yes, not only into my life but, as I gathered from his letter that night, into his as well. Two or three days earlier he had learned what he believed to be the full truth about Jakob's false, double life, a life based on a lie in which I had a substantial share. When his eyes were accidentally opened to what was going on between Jakob and me behind his back— he didn't say how or where or by whom—he felt that suicide was the only way out. I don't know if he overheard us together. It's also possible that other people gossiped about us. Then again, his own mother may have blurted out the truth in an unguarded moment. I used to think my wife naive, but now I'm not so sure she didn't know."

Erneste listened to the old man in silence. All it needed was another few words and his life would appear in a different light, a lackluster light that robbed everything of color and transformed his nostalgia for Jakob into the undignified whimpering of a dog that dreads its master's blows as much as it craves them. He could have risen with finality and brought Klinger's account to an end. He could have shaken off his lethargy and turned on the light, but he continued to sit and stare at the shadowy figure in front of him, which seemed to increase in size the more quietly it spoke and the faster the words escaped its lips, for Klinger was speaking faster now. The shadow seated in front of Erneste seemed to be engulfing everything around it, not least his own past and the still intact part of the picture he entertained of it.

"It was important to him to make me feel responsible for the act of self-destruction he would commit immediately after writing his letter. Only responsible? No, culpable. I should undoubtedly have felt guilty even if he hadn't accused me, because unlike him, Jakob and I were free agents. He was a captive. I wanted something from Jakob and got it, just as Jakob wanted something from me and got it. In many respects, and despite our interdependence, we were free—in a word, adults. But my son believed in love and exclusivity. He believed in Jakob.

"'Double life' and 'living a lie'—those were the two phrases that recurred in his farewell letter, an unmistakable echo of Ibsen, whose plays he had devoured as a youngster. He accused me of leading a double life in which he had no place. He hurled the same charge at his mother—at all of us, whom he regarded as members and beneficiaries of a conspiracy. He could neither go nor stay, he wrote—he couldn't move. Now that he'd seen through the lie into which we'd coerced him without his knowledge, he was finished, crushed, stifled. He had loved in secret and believed himself to be similarly loved in return, so how was he now, in retrospect, to evaluate that relationship? He'd deceived himself, he wrote, because he'd been deceived. He wondered what hold I must have had over Jakob to persuade him to give me his unconditional obedience, but he didn't ask *me* that question. He died believing that I'd had to put pressure on Jakob—that he'd *had* to give himself to me against his will. How greatly he loved him, and how little he knew him! He lacked the courage to raise the subject with Jakob. He was a coward like me—he couldn't discuss it with me either. He must have been utterly desperate during the few days before his suicide. If he'd tried to speak to me, I would have been able to enlighten him. But perhaps he wouldn't have believed me, and who knows, I might have denied the whole thing. After all, wasn't I jealous? Jealous and vain? A coward? I learned from Maxi's letter that Jakob had seduced him back in Giessbach. At the age of seventeen, guileless but not guiltless, Maxi had been unresistingly seduced at the same time as Jakob seduced and enslaved me—at the same time as you and he were sharing a room together. A room and a bed, perhaps an ideal conception of love."

So Jakob had been nimbly moving from one to the other, from father to son and from him to still others, bewitching and tempting them all.

"When Maxi made the unbearable discovery that his own father had been deceiving him with the person he loved most, the person who was, as he put it, his 'hold on life', his world promptly collapsed. He believed I knew about his tendencies—he thought I'd employed Jakob and taken him with us for his sake. And then, quite suddenly, it transpired that I hadn't employed Jakob to enable Maxi to lead a carefree existence, but in my own interests—'as ever', he wrote. The fact is, it would never have occurred to me that Jakob's relationship with my son was other than that of a servant. I'd stolen his lover, and he couldn't live with that thought. Yes, I understand him."

Klinger seemed to have reached the end of his account, the end of a story in which Erneste had had no part except in one respect: the "ideal conception of love" of which Klinger had spoken, but which had really been no more than an abortive attempt to be loved. But Erneste hadn't killed himself—he'd never even contemplated it.

All he could see of Klinger's eyes were the whites. The irises, eyelids and lashes had merged with the background in front of which he was sitting, slightly hunched but defiant, as if he might jump up at any moment. Erneste could only surmise that Klinger was watching him. The man was clearly unrelieved that he had recounted and explained everything worth knowing, all that he had thought of again and again over the years. The light was still on in the house across the street. Erneste's neighbor hadn't turned it off, so it probably stayed on the whole time. He could see the light even though he was sitting with his back to the window. The light in the apartment opposite was reflected in a mirror on the wall behind Klinger.

Jakob's love for Erneste had been only of brief duration, but that was possibly the best that could be said for it, because Jakob had probably meant what he said while it lasted. *Et alors voilà qu'un soir il est parti, le Postillon de Longjumeau.* And then, from one day to the next, the handsome young postilion had left.

———————

Klinger had been hard hit by his son's suicide. His unexpected insight into Maximilian's life had dealt him a blow which only a counterblow could parry. He prepared to deliver it within hours despite knowing that he himself would be its target. The reasons for Maxi's death were enough to warrant throwing Jakob out. He had to get rid of him. Whether he would succeed in effacing him from his memory was temporarily unimportant. Time would tell.

He sent for him before breakfast—even before he had seen anyone else. Jakob was looking wretched, and he looked more wretched still when Klinger gave him notice. He denied nothing and uttered no word of protest, neither disputed his responsibility for Maximilian's death nor tried to change Klinger's mind—which might have been easier than it seemed to him at the time. Klinger imagined that he could punish Jakob for his son's death by committing an arbitrary act. If he couldn't invest that death with meaning, he could at least repay one injustice with another. Later he realized how petty and unreasonable he had been, but that was later, not then. Then, when there was nothing more to be done, he wanted to take effective action of some kind. If he could do nothing else, he could punish himself, and he didn't regret having done so, either then or later.

Isolated snowflakes were falling on that bright, sunny winter's morning. As fine and firm as grains of dust, they drifted slowly down onto a world inhabited by people ignorant of the misery of those who, high above their heads, were facing the dismal prospect of a day on which all was past redemption. Jakob stood in front of Klinger looking pale and exhausted, staring at the floor with his arms hanging limp at his sides. But Klinger looked past him at a window in the building opposite, where a young man was leaning perilously far out and doing something to a flagpole, although no flag could be seen.

He didn't mind what the others thought about his firing Jakob, who had been in his employ for so long, at this seemingly inappropriate juncture. Unlike Frau Moser,

Jakob wasn't an indispensable member of the household. He would simply not be there anymore, and it wasn't until much later that Klinger found time to be surprised that no one had ever asked him why he'd let Jakob go. Neither his wife nor his daughter ever inquired the reason, which implied that they already knew it.

He told Jakob to pack his things and leave the same day, the sooner the better. Then he handed him an envelope containing three months' salary. Jakob would make out, he was experienced and knew plenty of people. He left the apartment at noon. Nobody saw him off or bade him farewell, and he himself considered it superfluous to shake hands with anyone. Besides, the others were too busy restoring order where Maximilian's death had wrought disorder to give any thought to him.

That evening, however, Marianne Klinger informed her husband that Jakob had kept watch over their son all night. She had found him seated beside the bed, wide awake, when she went into Maxi's room at half-past seven. Until he became aware of her presence he appeared to be communing with the dead youth. "I got the feeling they had a language of their own," she said. That had been the last time Jakob's name was mentioned in Klinger's presence until the day Erneste called him and requested an interview.

Jakob's suitcase was a small one, and he was in no hurry. There was plenty of time before he left to pack his few possessions: two pairs of trousers, two jackets, two pairs of shoes, underwear and socks, toilet things and writing materials, papers and money. Erneste sat on the bed with his knees drawn up and watched him packing. He wanted to memorize his every movement, knowing that he would subsist on the recollection for a long time to come. The little suitcase was lying open on the bed. Erneste could easily have touched it with his toes, but he did nothing of the kind. Mute and motionless, he looked on while Jakob, pausing for thought occasionally, went back and forth between the bed and the wardrobe, fetching various things that had accumulated in the last few months. All those tokens of his presence disappeared into the suitcase until nothing was left—until he might never have existed. Jakob had stripped to his underpants. The room beneath the eaves was already sweltering. It wasn't eight o'clock yet, and the steamer for Interlaken didn't leave until eleven. He was about to embark on the longest journey he'd ever made.

Lying on the chair beside the washbasin were the clothes he would wear today, the day of his departure: a pair of white, lightweight slacks, a white cotton shirt, fawn socks and brown oxfords—all of them purchased on a recent trip to Interlaken like his smart leather suitcase, which he was packing with a care Erneste found surprising. The money for the suitcase and the new clothes had been provided by Klinger, who had sent Jakob to

Schaufelberger's department store with a blank check and instructions to get himself a decent outfit. Klinger had laid down no rules about his wardrobe, so he could wear whatever he chose.

Jakob had asked Erneste to accompany him on his shopping trip to Interlaken, and although Erneste was under no illusions about its purpose, he had agreed. And that was how, for the space of half a day, their old, unconstrained relationship, which chimed so well with the glorious weather, had returned like some long familiar friend.

Two young men strolling along the promenade . . . Two young men sitting in the Café Schuh . . . Erneste and Jakob said not a word about what lay ahead, not a word about their parting in three days' time, not a word about the journey to Marseille and the voyage to America, not a word about Klinger and what would be lost beyond recall. For as long as their excursion to cosmopolitan little Interlaken lasted, the immediate future didn't exist, nor did the next day or the day after that. They made their way along the lakeside promenade and through Interlaken's shopping streets, walking so close together that their shoulders, arms and hands brushed again and again, at first by chance but later, perhaps, intentionally. Neither recoiled at the other's touch. It was as natural as breathing, as walking itself. Erneste would have walked beside Jakob for years on end—on through Interlaken and other places on this and the other side of the world he knew. He shut his eyes while walking, and, in the dappled reddish gloom transfixed by the shafts of bright sunlight that impinged on his retinas, those years at Jakob's side passed in a flash, serene and untroubled. Just as they were strolling through the town side by side, so they could have journeyed together down the years.

It was a dream, and Erneste managed to sustain it until they boarded the little steamer that took them back to Giessbach late that afternoon—for far longer, at any rate, than he had hoped at the start of their brief day's journey into the past. During the return trip across the lake, however, anguish overcame him with a ferocity that undid all his recent experiences: walking together, shopping at Schaufelberger's, regaling themselves in the Café Schuh with Black Forest gâteau and coffee followed by a shandy apiece. Now, even Jakob seemed to have ceased to exist. He was already as remote as if he had been ousted from Erneste's world at a stroke, even though, when Erneste opened his eyes, Jakob was still sitting there beside him, engrossed in thoughts to which he no longer had access. He couldn't help fearing that those thoughts had ceased to be of him and were now of Klinger. For all that, however, Jakob had accomplished what he'd probably had in mind when asking Erneste to keep him company: a kind of reconciliation. To all appearances, therefore, it was as if Erneste hadn't taken his infidelity amiss—as if he accepted it as a part of his character and an indispensable step into the future.

He would have liked to ask Jakob a simple question, but he didn't. It was far too late for simple questions like those that had haunted him for days. The question he dared not ask, because he dreaded a rebuff, was whether he could come with him to America. He, Erneste, at Jakob's side in America . . . There must surely be a place for him in Klinger's household, or, if not there, with one of the many other German families that were emigrating to America and had jobs to offer.

But he didn't ask, neither on the trip back to Giessbach, nor during the night that followed, nor during the very last night they spent together, when neither of them refused the other. Even as they were responding to each other with every fiber of their bodies, the words refused to be uttered by Erneste's inner voice, which kept urging him to ask Jakob if he could accompany him as the valet of a valet or secretary or lover, or whatever function or disguise Jakob was adopting in order to go away with Klinger. The opportunity didn't arise. He couldn't speak of it, and the simple, gnawing question lodged deep inside him, where it found the noxious sustenance on which it would feed for decades to come.

At last, when Jakob had stowed everything away in his suitcase, he went and stood at the washbasin with his back to Erneste. He bent and sluiced his face under the faucet, moistened his hair and sleeked it down. Taking the washcloth, he soaped it and swabbed his neck, shoulders, armpits and chest. He soaped it again and swabbed his stomach and back, insofar as he could reach it. Then he slid his underpants down over his thighs with his left hand, spreading his thighs a little to prevent them from slipping off, and used his right hand to soap his buttocks and genitals. Having wrung out the washcloth, he proceeded to wipe off the soap and dried himself carefully on a towel. He was smiling when he turned to face Erneste once more and started to get dressed.

If Erneste could have suited himself he would have stolen away after that, but he couldn't; he had to fulfill his promise to help Jakob with the baggage. Together, they conveyed the wardrobe trunk and the other pieces of luggage from the four rooms occupied by the Klingers and Frau Moser down to the lobby and from there, with the aid of a baggage cart, to the cable car.

The steamer left at eleven. While Klinger, his wife and two children looked back at the landing stage as if trying to preserve a vivid recollection of the place in Europe where they had spent a considerable period, possibly for the last time, Jakob gazed ahead at the mirror-smooth surface of the lake. Erneste was thus spared a final look into his eyes.

Muffled up in his heavy overcoat, he stared out across the lake. Just in front of him two swans were slowly swimming in circles, half submerging and surfacing in turn, and when they shook their heads the spray flew from their white necks, which looked as if they were covered with fur, not feathers. It was cold and windy, but the snow had stopped.

He had never paused there before in all the years he had lived and worked in this town and walked along the lakeshore almost daily, but now he came to a halt and looked out across the water. He sat down on a bench and stared straight ahead, but the far shore could not be seen, having vanished into the mist. In the middle of the lake, still just visible, was a little white steamer with white smoke rising from its black smokestack.

How many hours, days and weeks had gone by since then? He didn't bother to count. It didn't matter how much time had passed since that Sunday in October when Julius Klinger had called on him to tell him about Jakob, the lover of three men and of many more whose names they fortunately hadn't known—Jakob, who had died far away in a place to which Erneste would never travel and from which his last news of Jakob had come: cries for help that had swiftly faded because they were voiceless and incorporeal, just lines of writing on flimsy paper, a reverberation from the soundbox of some indeterminate instrument.

Klinger had eventually risen and stepped forward as if intending to kiss him, but Erneste had evaded him. No, no, it would have been too ridiculous to be kissed by that old man. It wasn't hostility, just old age, that made him recoil. He felt no hostility, for what had happened had happened long ago, at a time on which the curtain had now descended. At this moment it was as invisible as the far shore, as unfamiliar as the instrument from which Jakob's voice was issuing like a whisper. He had to be prepared for the mist soon to clear, disclosing the view once more, but more time would have passed by then.

Alain Claude Sulzer was born in Basel in 1953. His first novel was published in 1983 and he has since written four further books, including numerous short stories, and the novels *Annas Maske* (2001) and *Privatstunden* (2007). *A Perfect Waiter* (*Ein Perfekter Kellner*, 2004) is his first novel to be translated into English. He lives in Alsace.

———

John Brownjohn is one of Britain's leading translators from German and has won critical acclaim on both sides of the Atlantic, notably for *"My Wounded Heart": The Life of Lilli Jahn 1900–44* by Martin Doerry. Among his awards are the Schlegel-Tieck Prize for Thomas Brussig's *Heroes Like Us* and the Helen and Kurt Wolff Prize for Marcel Beyer's *The Karnau Tapes*.

The text of this book is set in Centaur. Centaur was designed by Bruce Rogers in 1914 as a titling fount only for the Metropolitan Museum of New York. It was modelled on Jenson's roman.